Jane Austen
Lied to Me

Jeanette Watts

To Dorothy -
You are such an awesome playmate!
Looking forward to going to the JASNA
event with you & Joan! We are going
to have a blast together!!
Here's to many adventures together
in the future.
♡,
Jeanette

To Brittany, Bunny, Dale, David, Jen, John, Justine, Karla, Katie, Ken, Larissa, Lon the Floor Nerd, Matt, Michael, Michelle, Natalie, Nathan, Paul, Tiffany, and Wendy. I hope you were amused by your "cameos."

And most importantly to Jane with profound admiration and gratitude..

FRESHMAN YEAR

Names hold an incredible amount of power. When parents name their children, they think they're just picking a name they like. Or pleasing their parents by naming the grandchildren for grandma or grandpa. What they don't realize is, when they choose a child's name, they are picking a personality – and forming their child's destiny.

All Michaels are full of the devil. All Johns can be kind of a jerk. All Franks are talkers. Saras without the "h" have a different personality than Sarahs with the "h." Avoid the Saras without "h's." Trust me on this.

My name is Elizabeth Barrett. Elizabeths do great things. But that has nothing to do with how or why I got my name. My mother loved Elizabeth Barrett Browning's poem, "How do I love thee? Let me count the ways" so much, she had to marry my dad because his last name was Barrett. And that's why she named me Elizabeth.

Which is sad, because it's a stupid poem. But then again, all poetry is stupid. Mom hates it when I say that. She can keep her Keats and Browning, and all the rest of the Romantics. I know how to find the good stuff.

I am what is commonly known as a Janeite. People who have watched the BBC movie of *Pride and Prejudice* with Colin

Firth and Jennifer Ahle a whole bunch of times think that qualifies them as a Janeite. That's pathetic.

I've read *Sanditon*, and *Love and Friendship*, and *Lady Susan* over and over so many times, I could write the Trivial Pursuit-Jane Austen edition. I own a copy of her letters, I own several biographies of her, both DVD documentaries and print versions.

I love that my name is so close to Elizabeth Bennett's. I tried to get my family and friends to call me Lizzie when I started high school, but you know how family is. My sister will use it sometimes – when she wants something from me. Everyone at school has been calling me Beth since first grade (which I don't mind too much, I love Louisa May Alcott, too). There's no getting my friends to change.

Being a freshman in college, I finally get my chance. I can introduce myself as Lizzie, and who is to say otherwise? I could tell people my name is Myrtle, or Sapphire, or Electra. I finally have some control over what people call me.

It's nice having some part of my life where I feel I have some level of control. So much of life seems to be one long exercise in parental appeasement. I'm going to the college they want me to attend, signed up for the classes they want me to sign up for, majoring in pharmacology because that's what they want me to do. They run a nursing home, and with a degree in pharmacology, I'll be able to fit right into the family business when I get out of school.

It's a shame they won't be able to check my homework for me anymore. At least I liked chemistry in high school. I'm glad there's no pharmacy program at the community college that's half an hour from our house. They would have insisted I live at home, so we could save money. I have enough in scholarships and loans to pay for the dorm as well as my tuition. I wish I would have started some sort of savings thing when I was five years old, but, oh well. At least I'm here, and presumably when I get out I'll make enough at my parents' nursing home to pay off the debts without much trouble.

Aug 27

I love my dorm! This is like a giant slumber party. My roommate is a girl named Anne (isn't that perfect? Like Anne from *Persuasion*). She's tall, and blonde, and even though she's tall she wears these really high heels. I like cute shoes just fine, but wow, she wears them all the time and she has an entire shoe rack to hang over her closet door. She let me try hers on because we have the same-sized feet. I found out that three inch spike heels do not make me feel sexy. They make me feel like I'm six years old wobbling around in my mother's heels.

"How on earth do you go up and down stairs in these things?" I asked her.

"That's what elevators are for," she laughed at me.

My parents and brother and sister, and her parents and younger sister all helped us move in, made the beds and put clothes in the closets and dressers. Then they cried over us, and kissed us goodbye, and made us promise to call home; but I could tell both of us could hardly wait until they were gone. Finally they left. We both wiped away some suspicious wet spots in our eyes, grinned at each other, and I knew I was right. I taped up my movie posters of *Sense and Sensibility* and *Pride and Prejudice* – and my posters of Colin Firth. I helped Anne tape up posters of The Beatles, The Who, and The Rolling Stones.

"Wow, so you think we're both Anglophiles?" I said, admiring her posters.

"I think we're going to get along just fine," she agreed. "So, now that we're both mostly unpacked, want to go exploring around the dorm a little more? I wouldn't mind finding the vending machines that we passed in the hall behind the elevators. I could use a Coke right now."

"Heck yah, I'll join you!"

Our dorm floor has girls on one side of the elevator, and guys on the other side of it. Almost everyone had their door open, and people were carrying stuff in, saying good-bye to parents, putting things away, and wandering around checking the place out, just like we were. There's a small lounge on each floor across from the elevators with a TV, tables with lamps on them and a bunch of comfy couches. There's a bigger lounge on the first floor. We were pleased that we were only three doors down from the bathroom. It would really suck to be at the far end of the hall, although we had to admit the extra windows in the end rooms were kind of nice. The RA lives in one of them.

We had just flopped down with our cokes in the comfy chairs in our floor's lounge when Anne's phone rang. It was her mom, already giving her advice about pledging for a sorority. I could tell it was starting to turn into a fight, and I was glad when she rolled her eyes at me and got up to walk out of the room.

"Well, that was kind of awkward, I'm glad she left," said a guy in the lounge, sitting at one of the tables with his laptop. He was blonde, and had glasses, and, well, all I could think was that he was like the classic definition of nerd from that old movie. All he needed was a geeky laugh, and he would be the perfect caricature.

"What do you mean?" I wasn't sure if I needed to be defending my new roomie or not.

"Arguments are kind of private." He looked at me. "Weren't you feeling a little uncomfortable listening to her fighting?"

"Well, now that you mention it, yeah, I was," I admitted.

We chatted for a while about cell phone manners, then he asked me my name. For the second time (the first time being with Anne), I got to do it. I told him my name is Lizzie.

"Hi, Lizzie. I'm Lon. Are you done moving in already? Want to go get some dinner or something?"

I think I stared at him blankly for a second. "Are you asking me out on a date?"

He looked calmly back at me. "Yes, I guess I am."

"Um, thanks, but no." I didn't want to tell him he wasn't my type. I didn't know what my type was, but I did know he wasn't it. I just wasn't interested. And let's face it, he was moving kind of fast. Asking me out after a ten minute conversation? No way.

Well, at least I can say that college is definitely an adventure!

Aug 31

The adventure continues…it turns out it's a good thing my parents insisted on bringing me an alarm clock, instead of using my phone as an alarm. My phone didn't charge overnight, and so it died at some point in the middle of the night. If it wasn't for Anne

5

getting up for her class, I would have slept through mine! Now I'll set both alarms. I suppose I ought to admit to my folks that they were right. My brother, David, and my sister, Wendy, and I all thought that they were being silly and old fashioned.

"No one under 30 uses an alarm clock," Wendy told them.

"No one under 25 uses an alarm clock," David corrected her. It was a new experience having both my siblings stand up for me. It's nice that they're excited for me. Or maybe they're just happy that I'm gone, and Wendy gets our room all to herself now. She's a junior in high school, so she'll be leaving, too, soon. That's probably what David is really excited about. Having both of us gone. He's only nine, so he'll have mom and dad to himself for a while.

My mom just smiled. "Humor me."

At least my first class isn't that far from my dorm. I slipped on a bra under my t-shirt, smoothed down my pajama pants a little, brushed my hair, and I was able to run there in something like five minutes. I've already decided I'm going to live on campus my whole college career. Living in an apartment off campus, needing a car and taking longer to get to class, and spending more money to be able to do so, is not a good use of either time or money.

I think I only missed the first ten minutes or so of biology class. Thank goodness it was the lecture part, not the lab part. That probably would have been much more awkward to be late for. The professor must have been quick with his opening announcements and whatever, because he already had a fair amount of stuff scribbled on the giant dry erase boards. I just plopped open my notebook and started taking notes on the sketch he was working on at the moment.

I felt lost and behind the entire lecture. I'm definitely going to be using that alarm clock my parents made me get. At least most of my classes don't start very early. It's really nice that, unlike high school, you get some choice in when you take classes. Biology is the earliest one I have to take. Biology lab, statistics, Spanish, and freshman composition are all later in the day. The first classes are for my pharmacology major, the writing class is required for all incoming freshmen, and the Spanish class is for me. I liked it in high school, and compared to all the other classes, it sounds fun and relaxing. Part of college is to round out one's education, right? Well, I figured Spanish will help me be educated and well rounded.

Sept 5

Well! That was interesting. My roommate invited me along to this frat party she was going to. She went through something called rush week, and she is now pledged to a sorority. She said the frats are less formal than the sororities, and even though I wasn't a pledge I could go with her. I figured, why not, it should be fun, right?

I got to meet the guy she's chasing. I couldn't blame her for being interested. He's cute, and sweet, and considerate, and a total people-pleaser. One of his parents must be the demanding sort who is never happy.

He introduced us to his friend... whose name is Darcy Fitzwilliam! I wasn't sure at first that the guy wasn't just pulling our legs.

"Your mother obviously loves Jane Austen," I laughed.

"Obviously," he answered. Not much to go by.

"I love *Pride and Prejudice*," I continued.

"I hate *Pride and Prejudice*," I can only describe the look he was giving me as hostile.

"I think you will find yourself very much in a minority," I answered, returning his look with one of my own.

We didn't talk any more that night. Talk about getting off on the wrong foot!

Sept 7

Today I got a flash of insight of what it's probably like for a guy with a name like Darcy Fitzwilliam...

In Spanish class, the teacher broke us up into little groups so we could practice our new vocabulary. She doesn't want us partnering with the same people all the time, so she folded the alphabet in half. Since Barrett puts me at the top, I was paired with a "W" from the other end of the roster.

She read off our full names from her roster, so I didn't get to introduce myself. So until I can correct them, the class thinks my name is Elizabeth. Or, at least my partner thought so when we paired up.

"Elizabeth Barrett? Hi, I'm Bryan Woldseth. So, how do I love thee? Shall I count the ways?"

If I had a dime for every time I've had that stupid poem recited to me, I could stack them all up, glue them together, and use them to pole jump to the moon. I just smiled at him. "Only if you count them in Spanish." I mean, really, do people think they're being original?

That's when it struck me. Darcy must hate *P&P* about as much as I hate "How Do I Love Thee?"

Now, if he had any manners, he would have found something less rude to say. Find a way to talk around it, instead of being a jerk. Since I'd just established that I love *Pride and Prejudice*, he could have said more about his mother. "My mother owns six copies of it." Or, "Most people do." Or hell, even, "Yeah, I get that a lot." But really, to just bluntly say he hates it while giving me the death glare is a bit much.

Wow. He really is just like Jane Austen's Mr. Darcy.

Sept 19

Mr. Fitzwilliam (I can't call him Darcy! It's a sacrilege, somehow) turned up at Anne's sorority party today. What a nice way to ruin my day…

The party started out nicely enough. Lots of dancing and Long Island Iced Teas. I had a couple more than I should have, but who doesn't? They're Long Islands.

Eventually I realized Darcy (damn! I mean Mr. Fitzwilliam) was there. And he was staring at me. I can only assume he doesn't drink, and doesn't approve of drinking. I've got news for him then, he'd better stay away from frat and sorority parties.

Some of Anne's sorority sisters are really on my case to become a pledge. I really do like them, but it takes money to belong to a sorority. I was pretty successful at dodging the sales pitches, by distracting them with more booze or more dancing.

I was feeling a little bit wobbly later in the evening. I wasn't completely plastered, by any stretch of the imagination, but I'd certainly had a few.

I was crossing the room to return my empty glass, when I nearly tripped. Anne's sorority sister, Linda, caught me before I could fall.

"Time for you to slow down a little bit – maybe you should get a glass of water for your next round?" she said to me.

"Maybe I will. I should be leaving soon anyway. The walk home will clear my head," I answered.

Linda frowned. "You're not walking home alone, are you?"

"Well, I don't think Anne is ready to leave yet, but I've got class in the morning. She doesn't."

"Well, we'll just have to find you an escort, then." She turned around and tapped the arm of the man behind her. "Darcy, would you be willing to play escort for a little while? Our guest needs a ride home."

"I'm just across campus, it's not a long walk," I demurred.

"Incidents still happen. No one is going to get assaulted walking home after a party from this establishment," she said fiercely.

"I would be very happy to give the young lady a lift home," Darcy answered gravely.

Oh, God, I could tell I was right. He is some sort of teetotaler. Blech. "I wouldn't want to inconvenience this fine gentleman. I'm sure I'll find someone else here who is going to want to head back to my dorm soon."

"Nonsense! Darcy is always happy to show off his Bimmer to anyone willing to be his audience."

"If I'm drunk enough that I throw up in his BMW, I would never be able to forgive myself. No, I will find another way home," I answered, and beat a hasty retreat before Linda could prevail upon either me or him any longer.

I spotted Lon, the floor nerd from my dorm. What an incredible bit of luck. Was it tacky to press gang someone into service after I said no, I wouldn't go out with him? Maybe. I was desperate enough that I didn't care. And I was betting I could count on him to come to my aid. "Come on, you're walking me home, right now," I took his arm in a death grip and marched him toward the door.

"Sure," he answered. "Are you okay?"

"If I have to throw up on the walk back, then we'll know I'm not okay. If we make it to the dorm without incident, we'll declare me 'okay.' Do those seem like reasonable enough terms?"

"Sure," he answered.

I got home without throwing up then, or ever. I've never been so drunk I've thrown up. I don't think I ever want to be that drunk. Or, maybe I was so drunk I not only threw up, I also didn't remember anything. So I wouldn't remember the throwing up part.

Without any eyewitnesses, I'll just assume the former. Of course, if the eyewitnesses were also so drunk they don't remember what happened, they won't be reliable eyewitnesses.

So, I guess I'll never know. Unless I ask Lon. But I'm afraid if I ask him, he might ask me out again. I know geeks are in right now, but... no. I'm not following that fashion trend.

Sept 21

There's this favorite spot in the library where the friends I've met in biology like to hang out. It's got a large assortment of comfy chairs, and tables, and funny little round things that can be used as chairs or tables. It's well lit, and carpeted, and the space is just brilliant. You can go there to work on homework, or to take a nap between classes, or to hang out with your friends. All of the above is always going on at the same time.

It's my favorite spot on the whole campus. Almost any time I walk past, I know someone in "our" spot. Or a couple of someones. It's not unusual for eight of us to all be sitting there, dragging over more chairs, laughing, talking, showing some post that the rest of us haven't seen yet.

Today I was the first one on the scene, and was actually getting my homework done. I have a huge pile of reading to do. Then Frank and Tiffany showed up with this box of cards. At first I declined to play, and pulled my chair over to the side a little. Then Dale and Allie showed up and they all started reading these cards. They kept pestering me to play. I promised I would as soon as I finished the chapter I was reading.

Meanwhile, who should show up, but the guy that Anne has been chasing around, and Darcy Fitzwilliam! Anne's amour knew Dale and Allie, and next thing you know the two of them are pulling up chairs and hanging out with my crowd.

I mean, really? There's just no getting away from this guy.

I realized I was now reading the same paragraph over and over again, because I was irritated by the addition to our group. Time to give it up and either go someplace else to read, or join in the game.

Naturally the moment I closed my book, Tiffany handed me a bunch of cards. Okay, so I'm playing the game.

I had to read a question, and then a bunch of possible answers, and I had to pick my favorite answer, and then say why. When I made my choice, there was a flurry of protests.

"No, way! You don't really think that brains are more important than beauty, do you?"

"One lasts, the other doesn't," I defended my choice.

"Not if you get Alzheimer's."

"That's not until years after beauty is already gone."

"So you're saying beauty is only on the surface?" Mr. Fitzwilliam asked. "Isn't that a rather shallow definition of beauty? You don't think that someone can be beautiful from within? Or that it's possible to be an 80 year old woman with a beautiful soul, or mind, or some such?"

"I'm talking about physical beauty, I wasn't trying to get into a philosophical discussion on the nature of truth and beauty."

"But part of the point of this game is to get into discussions, philosophical and otherwise. It makes people look inside themselves."

"I didn't bother to look inside myself, I just took the card at face value."

"Pun intended?" I could see Darcy – I mean Mr. Fitzwilliam – was smirking, and trying not to look amused.

"The subconscious ones are always better, anyway," I answered sarcastically. "Stop trying to show off. Okay, you're a witty guy. No one's going to dispute that."

I realized my friends were kind of looking at me, but I couldn't help myself. His superior little attitude was annoying me.

"You're depriving us of your full wit, if you're only giving us subconscious puns instead of really applying your brain to your conversations. You should pay more attention to life around you. If you're always someplace else, you're going to miss a lot."

Allie interrupted us at that point, and shoved a group of cards into Mr. Fitzwilliam's hand. "Okay, okay, too much blather, not enough playing. If my mother was here, she'd say 'No more arguing about the last round.' Your turn to pick now."

Sept 23

The new assignment in Spanish class is to write a scene. I got paired with a guy named Ken. This could be promising; Ken is a little short, but kind of cute. In a ROTC kind of way. Which is weird, for a shorter guy. But it works. He's got really strong-looking shoulders.

Ken and I met at Starbucks to work on our scene. I like a guy who is as addicted to coffee as I am! We had gotten around to dispensing with idle chitchat and focusing on the project. So far we'd brainstormed the ideas of either a love scene or some sort of horror zombie kind of scene when Mr. Fitzwilliam walked into the shop.

If I try to be objective, I guess he is kind of good-looking. Not in a ROTC way. He's more the GQ type. I don't think GQ models ever smile, either.

Ken saw me staring and turned to see what I was looking at. Which, of course, staring at him drew Fitzwilliam's attention to the two of us.

I was a little surprised when the two guys looked at each other with undisguised dislike. Neither one of them said anything, and then Fitzwilliam (man, that's just too much to write out every time! I'm going to have to start calling him Fitz) moved past us to go order at the counter.

"You know that guy?" I asked Ken.

"Yeah, we were on the wrestling team together in high school. He's a real douchebag," Ken muttered.

"I got that impression, too," I told him. "So can we use him as the star of our scene? A guy being a real dickhead?"

"You know, that might work. We'll call it 'a scene from real life,' " Ken answered.

We got our scene written before our coffees even had a chance to get cold.

Oct 10

I am not – repeat – not going to join Anne's sorority. Not if it ends up making me like Anne. I went with her and another pledge to this sorority function off campus, and in a fit of irresponsibility or something, they went off without me!

When I realized how late it was, and I texted her to ask "Where are you?" she didn't even have the grace to be embarrassed. She just wrote "OMG, forgot U came with us, can U find a lift home?"

Linda the sorority sister must really have it out for me, or really wants to play matchmaker; wouldn't you know it, she spotted my plight and once again foisted Darcy Fitzwilliam on me!

I was talking to a girl I didn't know to see if she was heading back towards campus anytime soon, when Fitz walks up to us and interrupts us, saying "Linda told me you are in need of a lift. I was about to leave. Are you ready to go? I'll get you home."

I opened my mouth to say I had just worked out a ride, but the girl looked at Fitz and said, "Thank you, that would be awesome. Then I don't have to clear out a space in my car." Then she left me standing there, sort of blinking at Fitz.

"Let's go, then." He took my arm by the elbow in this courtly 'ushering his lady' sort of maneuver. It was some sort of evil trick, because while my mouth was forming the word no, my feet started walking with him.

He really does drive a Bimmer. A very nice Bimmer. Whatever his daddy does, he does it really well.

He opened the car door for me, and while my brain said, "No, thank you," my body obediently got in the car. I'll give it points for pragmatism. I really did need a ride home, after all, and I didn't exactly know many people at the function. So I sat there thinking about how I was going to wring Anne's neck when I get home.

He got in next to me, put the key in the ignition, and we were off. His car hums like a happy refrigerator, or something else inanimate that hums. It's got a smooth ride, incredibly comfy seats, and very little road noise.

Which quickly became awkward, since neither of us said anything. At least if we'd been riding in a noisy pickup truck with the windows rolled down, we wouldn't have needed to talk. But the silence was maddening.

"We can't spend the entire trip saying absolutely nothing," I pointed out.

"I'd assumed that after being deserted by your friends, you weren't going to be much in the mood for conversation," he answered.

Oh, so he's putting it on me, huh? That irritated me. "I suppose you're thinking that I need to improve my taste in friends," was what popped out of my mouth.

"And boyfriends. Are you and Ken dating?"

I was surprised by the question. "No, he's my partner for a project in my Spanish class. The teacher did this game where we all drew names from Spanish literature and culture, and we had to walk around finding the matching name. It was fun. The teacher really likes mixing it up, and being random whenever possible."

"Good. If he asks you out, be on your guard. At home, there are a lot of girls out there with his face on their dartboards."

The idea! As if girls tended to have dartboards in their bedrooms. This guy doesn't quite live in the real world. But then, look at what he's driving. He probably went to boarding school in England and spent his childhood foxhunting or yachting. Maybe his sisters all have dartboards. "You like to give out dating advice a lot? Or only when talking about Ken?" I asked.

"If I ever meet anyone else like Ken, I will warn women about him, too," he answered stiffly, then didn't say much more on the rest of the drive back to campus.

"Thank you for the lift, I appreciate you coming to my rescue," I said when he stopped the car. Just because he doesn't have much in the way of manners doesn't mean I'm going to neglect to use mine. I really expected to jump out at the curb, but he parked the car, got out, came around, and opened the door for me. Which was actually kind of nice, since the car is low to the ground, and he gave me a hand to help pull me up out of the seat. So, he's showing that he has manners, too. Whatever.

After he pulled me up, we stood there a second, our right hands still connected in a handshake. So, I shook his hand. "Thanks again," I said, and then I extricated myself, feeling a little gross for being beholden to someone I really don't like. It's kind of a nasty feeling.

Oct 29

I finally found out the name of that guy that Anne is chasing around. It's Phil. I ran into him today at our favorite library spot. Friendly guy. It was nice, I didn't know his name, he didn't know mine, but he had a nice way of asking me, and introducing himself, without being awkward, since it seemed like we ought to know each other's names by now. We were laughing and talking, when I realized that Fitz was lurking around in the background. Oh, that's right. These two guys are friends. Kinda weird, talk about opposite dispositions. I suppose the expression "opposites attract" might work for friends as well as lovers. Or maybe these guys are gay lovers – which makes some sense. Anne doesn't seem to be getting anywhere with Phil. Maybe Phil doesn't swing that way, and that's why he hasn't asked her out yet.

Finally I got tired of seeing Fitz lurking and glaring in the background, and I pointed him out to Phil. "I think your friend is waiting for you."

Phil turned around. "Hey, Darce." Then he looked at me, then back at him. "Wait, are you that Lizzie? The one he drove home from the party the other day? With the flighty friend?"

"Yes," I answered warily, wondering what else Fitz might have told him.

"The flighty friend who ditched you – was that Anne?"

As mad as I'd been at Anne for forgetting me, I didn't want to admit it to him. It didn't put her in a good light, and I knew she was really into this guy. I couldn't mess up her chances with him, if she had any, but I couldn't think of anything else to say. "Yeah, it was," I said. Then I had an inspiration. "Someone had told her they saw me leave with someone else, so she didn't think I was still there," I lied. "It was kind of a mess, but what do you do? No harm done." Oh, you owe me big time, Annie girl, I thought to myself. Fitz was still staring at me, which goaded me into adding out loud, "Except that Mr. Fitzwilliam thinks I have really irresponsible friends."

That seemed to spur him to action. He stepped up beside Phil and said to me, "I trust you've talked to your friend and let her know she needs to be more responsible in the future?"

"Of course," I lied. "It was only a little miscommunication. It's funny to think these things happen, even when we've all got cell phones glued to our persons and everybody can talk to each other 24/7."

That seemed to be the extent of Fitz's language skills, and he went back to looking at me while Phil and I talked. Now that he was doing it up close, it made me really uncomfortable, so I pretended I had to get to class, and left.

Nov 7

I am never, never accepting an invitation to anything, ever again. I mean it. Lon invited me to go with him to a LAN party.

They were playing a game I play at home with my brother David, so I figured, sure, why not?

The "why not" is because the party turned out to be at Darcy Fitzwilliam's house! I should have figured it out as soon as we walked in the door. The party wasn't in student housing. It was in a very nice place off campus. Lon was driving. It was dark, and I didn't pay that much attention to where we were going. I was worrying a little about whether Lon was going to think this was some kind of date. Because I'm really, really not interested in him.

I should pay more attention to my surroundings. Next thing I know, we're in this giant living room/dining room sort of space with tall ceilings. I claim a space at this monster dining room table, and find an empty power outlet on the power bar to plug in my laptop. I'm powering up when in walks Phil, carrying a bunch of bags of munchies he dumps in the middle of the table. "Hey, Phil! Small world!" I greeted him.

"It's an even smaller world than that," he said to me with a laugh. "I think you know our host, Darcy?"

He gestured behind me. I turned around. And sure enough, there was Darcy, setting up drinks and ice on the credenza against the wall.

Oh, dear God. I didn't think the guy would do anything so current as play a video game. Or as sociable as hosting a LAN party!

"Miss Barrett, I'm delighted you could join us," he greeted me with his usual demeanor – sort of reminiscent of the director at a funeral home, with a penchant for bizarrely formal language.

"Mr. Fitzwilliam, thank you for inviting me, although I suppose Lon's really the one who invited me." If he can be all formal and polite, I can do it, too.

"I asked him to find an eighth player, I didn't know he knew you – or that you played. I would have invited you myself had I known," he answered with his weird combination of rudeness and a sort of irritating gallantry.

"The way we keep running into each other, I think you can safely assume that I know who you know, and I do the same things you do. Eventually we'll find areas of life where we don't intersect, but it will save us time and trouble," I suggested.

"Where do you two know each other from?" Lon asked us, with enough of a catch in his voice to tell me my suspicions were correct, and he did indeed have "designs upon me," as they used to say.

"Oh, let's see, frat parties, sorority fundraisers, libraries, Starbucks, I'm expecting him to show up in my Spanish class any day now," I answered. "I think he's stalking me."

"Do I seem like the stalker type to you?" Darcy asked, one eyebrow having gone up. Damn him, I always wanted to be able to do the Mr. Spock one-eyebrow thing.

"You know what they say, you've got to watch out for the quiet ones," I said.

"It's not that I'm quiet, it's just…" Fitz started, and then stopped talking.

"It's just that you're a maniacal stalker? I think we've now established that," I joked.

"I'm not adept at talking to women," he confessed.

"Why would you have a hard time talking to girls?" I asked. "You've got money, looks, brains. What's not to like?"

"I don't know. I never seem to know what to say in mixed company."

"Have you ever tried, 'hello?' That usually seems like a good place to start," I answered. I meant to be sarcastic, but it came out much milder than I meant.

"Are you two going to flirt all night, or are we going to shoot things?" One of the other guys at the table finally jumped in. Damnedest thing about playing a game. There's no wondering what you're going to talk about. You talk about shooting things, duh...

Nov 19

I got a job! I'm at the circulation desk of the law library. So a whole lot of sleep-deprived caffeine junkies come hand me books that they want to take home and fall asleep over in their dorms, instead of at a library table. I put in applications all over campus, and tried to focus on jobs in the sciences that might be good experience for a future pharmacist. Not much luck on that score. I'm happy enough. This will do. It's a great job. I get to do my homework while getting paid at the same time. I'll just get interrupted sometimes to check out books, and spend some time reshelving them, which makes for a nice posture break from time to time. It doesn't get much better than this.

That's how I found out that Darcy Fitzwilliam is in law school. I should have figured. He's already perfected his poker face for the courtroom.

He came up to my desk and asked me a question, and I told him he really needed to speak to the reference librarian. "I'm only here to stamp the books after you pick them out. I don't field questions. I think you have to be a lawyer before you're qualified to be a reference librarian in a law library."

He went over to the reference desk, and I went back to the stack of books I was processing. I was a little startled when I got up from the desk to put my stack of books on a cart, and he was standing there again.

"Have you been working here long?" he asked me.

"I started Tuesday, so, no."

"Ah, that's why I haven't seen you here before." We stood there for a moment, looking at each other. I had my arms loaded down with books, he stood in between me and the cart where I could put them down. "Well, I'm sure I'll see you again." He walked away.

His eyes are brown.

Dec 7

I swear, there's never a dull moment at Starbucks.

I was sitting there at a table in the corner, minding my own business and getting my homework done with a big pumpkin spice latte with extra sugar, when in walks Fitz. And he's acting weird. I mean, he's acting weird even for him.

He saw me, and then ignored me, then obviously changed his mind and came over to my table. "No study partners today?" he asked me.

23

"No, all my work right now has to be done solo," I answered.

He nodded and kind of grunted a little, and then walked off. After he got his coffee, however, he came back over to my table. "May I join you?"

I was so weirded out by his bizarre request, I stammered, "Uh, sure, if I can make enough space for you." I mean, really, when a girl has her notes and books spread all over the top of the table, doesn't that sort of say, "Go sit someplace else?" My six-page final paper for freshman composition class was due on Wednesday, and I can't say it was going very well so far.

I pulled my things back enough so he had a place to put his coffee down. He sat there for a while, toying with his cup and watching me, then leaned forward to read my pages upside down.

"What's this, botany?"

I turned around the sheets of paper with sketches of flowers on the top of my stack. I was going to be polite to this guy if it killed me. "It's part of my freshman comp class. We're supposed to explicate something, so I'm writing about Louisa May Alcott and how the Victorians were into the language of flowers. You know, so honeysuckle stood for devotion, and lavender symbolized mistrust, and lilac expressed the first emotions of love."

"Sounds like an amusing project," he said gravely.

"I thought it would be, but it's turning out to be a lot more complicated than I thought. Everyone used to send coded messages using flowers, but there must have been a lot of regional dialects. I'm finding multiple dictionaries on the language of flowers. The same flowers don't always mean the same thing." I don't know why I was sharing my frustrations on writing this paper to him. I guess I was just looking for something – anything – to say to him. "I really get how all these languages worked. They were the leet of their time. Parents wouldn't know the code, just the kids, and so they were able to communicate secretly to each other, even with grownups standing right next to them."

"Sounds like this has become a bigger project than you were expecting." Again, that funny sort of courtly gravity about him.

"Yeah," I admitted. "There's a lot more to this than I thought. But I get plenty of study time while I'm sitting at the circulation desk."

"And when you're sitting in coffee shops," I think he was trying to smile at me.

"I have to get this done by tomorrow," I answered, hoping he'd get the hint. I don't think he did, because he didn't leave.

He toyed with his coffee cup some more, then said, "Look, this isn't my idea, but I need a date for my cousin's wedding during winter break. Phil's been telling my sister all about you, and now my whole family says they want to meet you. I told them all you're not the sort who would fit in with my family, but they're insistent. That is, if you have the means to come up with an appropriate dress these sorts of events require.

"I should warn you my family is probably not the same as yours in its expectations. So when I say a nice dress, I don't mean a used bridesmaid's dress from the thrift store or some off the rack thing from Sears. I don't suppose you have a friend or relative who can give you guidance on appropriate attire."

I couldn't believe my ears. Did he really just insult both my economic situation in life and my taste in clothes?

"Would you rather come over and look through my clothes to see if there's anything you might find acceptable?" I asked sarcastically.

"I don't have the time to tutor you on how to dress for a Long Island wedding," he answered. I couldn't tell if he got my sarcasm, and was answering with sarcasm of his own, or if he really thought it was unreasonable of me to make this demand upon his time.

I sat there for a moment, looking at him. "Well," he asked impatiently, "will you be my date for this wedding?"

I licked my lips and tried to figure out where to start. "Let me get this straight. You're asking me on a date because your family wants to look me over like a prize breeding cow. You expect me, my friends, and family to all go into what is for us an extreme amount of trouble, because you think it's some kind of special privilege for me to go on this date with you. You started by admitting that you didn't even want to ask me, but you're being coerced by your family. You also managed to throw in an insult to my taste in clothing, as if there's anything wrong with thrift store clothing. It just so happens I've seen $500 designer label clothing in my size at thrift stores. Most of the world shops at thrift stores, and we think it's fun. It's not even about the money, it's a sport. It's like fishing. I've heard sorority girls, who are probably richer than you, brag about clothes they're wearing that they got from thrift stores. And they're bragging because they got it for $1.50."

I stopped because I needed to take a breath, and then continued. "If you're so worried about being disgraced by me, why don't you find some girl to take to the wedding who won't embarrass you? I have no interest in meeting your family. You've made it very clear that I make poor eye candy, so I think you'd better look elsewhere."

"That's it?" he actually seemed surprised that I said no. "You really won't go with me?"

"No, Mr. Darcy Fitzwilliam, I won't go with you. You're an arrogant asshole. Now, go away, I've got a paper to write."

He stared at me for a second, still in disbelief I think, and then he got up and left. That is absolutely it. Lizzie Bennett was a moron. Rich jerks are not actually nice guys on the inside, once you get to know them better. I am through, absolutely through. Hopefully I was rude enough, and straightforward enough, that he'll make a point of avoiding me if he ever sees me again. I am certainly going to do my best to avoid him. And he'd better not ever need a library book checked out again. I will be marking it six years overdue since, after all, he can afford to pay the fines.

Dec 16

Thank goodness for Christmas break! My brain is full, and tired from all the course work, and then to top it all, I got to have an asshole ask me out in the most insulting way possible. For the most part I love being at college, but after that debacle, I'm glad I'm going home. I want my mother.

She picked me up an hour after my last final exam (would that be my final final?). Anne is already gone, she was done with her last exam 24 hours before I was. Lucky thing, she gets an entire extra day to get Christmas shopping done. I was still throwing my laundry into a duffel bag when Wendy knocked on the door. "Beth? I mean, Lizzie? You in there?"

"Wendy?" I squealed and ran to open the door. "Oh, it's good to see you!" I hugged her, and Mom. "I'm so glad to see you! Sorry I'm not ready yet. I've been totally focused on my exams until an hour ago."

The two of them helped me finish packing, then I showed them around the dorm a little. When I moved in, we were all pretty focused on the moving-in process. They didn't really see anything else then except my room and the freight elevator.

"Wow, it's like being at Hogwarts," my little sister cooed. I showed her the lounge on our floor, and the big common room downstairs before we left.

"Yeah, it kind of is like Hogwarts, but that was more like high school. High school isn't like college."

"Is it a lot more work than high school?" Wendy asked.

"You'll see when you get to college. They just pile it on, and pile it on. High school teachers talk to the other teachers so they know when the senior paper is due in English. Every college professor thinks they are the only class that's giving you a big assignment. They don't know and they don't care that every other class is giving you some giant paper due the same week. Midterms are insane, and with finals, they expect you to be superhuman or something."

"If you think that's hard, wait until you get out of school and face an entire nursing home full of sick patients," Mom said with a funny little smile. "Every single patient is like having an exam. You have to prove what you know, and know more than everyone else, because you're the expert on every drug. You can even countermand a doctor's orders, if there are drugs that don't interact well."

"Wow, Mom, no pressure," I said to her.

On the drive home, I talked about my roommate, and dorm life, and my classes, but I didn't tell them anything about Darcy and his invitation to his cousin's fancy wedding. I haven't decided how much of this I'm going to tell anyone. Mr. and Mrs. Bennett never knew anything about Lizzie's adventures – except for the Mr. Collins episode. I wouldn't let my mother set me up on a blind date, let alone pick a husband for me. Of course, Jane knew everything. But I'm not as close to Wendy as Lizzie was to Jane. Or, in real life, Jane was to her sister Cassandra.

Dec 31

I came home looking for reassurance, and for a reminder what life is like outside academia. I'd forgotten that when life isn't consumed by classes, and Greek parties, it's mostly about fights with siblings over clothes and space issues, and parents giving advice about stuff they don't know anything about, and doing chores like washing the dishes after dinner and taking out the garbage. At least it's also about happier things, like shopping, and wrapping presents, and decorating cookies, and Christmas dinner and getting a new Colin Firth poster under the tree.

Now it's New Year's Eve already. While our parents were out partying and we were home with the TV and pizza, I confided in Wendy and David about what happened with Darcy Fitzwilliam.

"He really drives a BMW?" David was all about the car. "Why didn't you just get a stupid dress, and lie to him and tell him it cost a million dollars, so you could ride with him out to this wedding? You could've ridden all the way to Long Island in a Bimmer!"

"You only talked with him in the first place because you liked his name," Wendy looked at me shrewdly. "Sounds like that didn't work out so well for you."

"Well, you've got to admit, Darcy Fitzwilliam is an awful lot like Fitzwilliam Darcy," I pointed out. "The resemblance goes deeper than just the name."

"Who cares if he's like the hero in your mushy movie? You blew the chance to ride all the way to Long Island in a Bimmer," David's priorities were clear. "I bet there will be all kinds of cool cars in the parking lot at the wedding."

"When you're older, you could be a valet, and you can park all those cool cars at weddings," I suggested.

His eyes got big. "I could so do that!"

I stared grumpily at him. "If I would have dated him, maybe eventually he would have bought me my own Bimmer. The rich guy in *Fifty Shades of Grey* bought the heroine a car, if I remember correctly."

David was now looking at me in disgust. "Wow, you really did blow it. Why did you turn this guy down?"

"Because he's a jackass." I answered.

"Is that really such a bad thing?" David asked.

"Yes, actually, it is," I told him.

"Well, then, you did the right thing," Wendy concluded confidently. I must say, I really do feel better having her validation on the subject.

Jan 29

Spring semester! I get to have a fresh start with new classes, new professors, and hopefully no Darcys to provide distraction and irritation. I still have my job at the law library circulation desk, so I probably won't be able to avoid seeing him from time to time. But after some time at home to clear my head, I'm ready to face him down.

My course schedule is going to be as busy this spring as it was in the fall. I have chemistry, and chem lab, and calculus, and Spanish 202, and just because I needed a gen ed requirement, I'm taking a class called Introduction to Western Philosophy.

It is so nice getting back to school! Anne is still all wrapped up in sorority stuff, Ken is still in my Spanish class, and Tiffany, Allie, and company still like to hang out at our sweet spot in the library. It's funny how I've only been at school for a few months, but it's already the new "normal" for me. I love never having to do dishes, and being surrounded by so many other people in the dorm. There is always something going on. And everyone has the same problem – trying to get the next class assignment done, on time and correctly.

Several of my friends from biology are taking the same chemistry class I am, and I think I'm going to be glad of it. Tonight I was feeling a little lost after the first week's lectures and homework assignments, so I grabbed my books and headed over to the library. I knew someone from our clan would be able to explain some of this stuff to me.

My heart sank as I approached our area. There was indeed one person I knew over in the sweet spot: that damn Darcy. He was pacing, lurking around. I stopped dead when I realized: in *Pride and Prejudice*, after Lizzie tells him off, he gives her a letter explaining himself.

I watched him while he was unaware of me, and I realized I didn't know what I was hoping for. Maybe it's more accurate that I was hoping for two opposite things. I hoped that he was lurking there because he knew that's where I hung out a lot, and he was there to give me some sort of explanation or apology. At the same time, I hoped that was totally not the case at all.

As I was thinking that rather than standing there like an idiot, the thing to do was turn around and walk away, that's exactly when Darcy spotted me.

Talk about awkward. I suppose I could have just turned around and run away, but I realized that was the wrong thing to do. He was the one standing in my favorite hangout spot. If I run away now, I'll have to run away from him every time I see him. And what do I do the next time I'm at the law library the same time he is? What would Lizzie Bennett do in this situation? She always met things head on. I had to do the same, and stand my ground.

I strode forward, forcing myself to move casually while I glanced around the library, looking to see if I knew anyone else there, then claiming an empty chair. I nodded a noncommittal greeting to him.

He nodded back at me, and continued to pace. So, maybe he wasn't lurking there for my benefit.

I tried to work on my chemistry homework, but I couldn't concentrate on anything else with Darcy hovering.

A little while later, a very skinny, yet at the same time buxom, blonde in a tight striped dress came sauntering into the tableau. She was Barbie incarnate.

"You're late," Darcy said to her irritably.

She laughed, wrapped an arm around him, and kissed him possessively. "I'm always late." He scowled at her, she ignored it and slipped her arm through his. "Thank you so much for taking me to your cousin's wedding during winter break," she purred. "I had a marvelous time."

I swear he threw a glance at me over his shoulder before they walked away. "I'm glad you enjoyed yourself," I heard him say as they walked out of earshot.

I stared at my homework in front of me, not seeing any of it. So, that was it, then. Instead of a letter, I'd gotten a message (in a manner that can only be described as a real dick move) that he easily replaced me with somebody else. No letters, no defense, no starting over.

This isn't going at all the way things did in *Pride and Prejudice*. Or, maybe things are going exactly as they did in *Pride and Prejudice*. I can't tell if we're still on script or off. I guess only time will tell.

The funny thing is, I don't want Mr. Fitzwilliam to turn out to be Mr. Darcy. I've had all I can stand of him. He's a jerk, an asshole, and I'm pretty firmly convinced that he isn't magically going to turn out to be a noble gentleman if you speak to his servants.

I threw everything into my backpack and headed back to the dorm. I wasn't going to get anything done, sitting there. I was also afraid that maybe Darcy would come back the same way, and I didn't want to see him twice in one night.

Feb 5

It's been a week, and I'm still bothered by seeing Darcy and the girl he took to the wedding. Even though I really should have spent tonight working on my chemistry homework, after class I threw myself on my bed with my copy of *Pride and Prejudice*, hoping I'd find a comforting passage. Maybe I'm not cut out to be Lizzie Bennett. I admire her, but am I as witty as she is? Do I have her sense of humor? Could I hold my own in a confrontation with someone as formidable as Lady Catherine DeBurgh? If I'm honest with myself, I think the answer to all those questions is no.

What would Jane's Lizzie have done if she were me, and confronted with Darcy Fitzwilliam? That's an interesting question: she would have done the same things I had. She did do the same things I did. He snubbed her, she found him annoying. He asked her to marry him (yes, I know it isn't quite the same as a date for a wedding) in the most insulting way possible. She told him to go fuck himself. Isn't that precisely what I did?

But this is where my story seems to be losing the narrative. In the book, Mr. Darcy cares enough about her to write her a long letter defending himself. Then he works on improving his manners, to prove he's not the jerk she takes him to be. In my life, my (huh) Darcy just moved on to someone else.

I guess it's too early to draw any conclusions yet. I'm going to have to wait and see what happens next. If I end up touring his house while he's supposed to be gone, and he goes out of his way to be pleasant, then maybe I'm still living the story. After all, I'm likely to see him at the law library from time to time. In a way, it's kind of a cognate for being at Pemberley. I'm on his turf.

Feb 22

It has only taken me a month to figure out that this semester is going to suck. Spanish is fine, and I'm really, really enjoying the Intro to Western Philosophy class, but chemistry and chem lab are nothing like they were in high school. I constantly feel like I'm behind, not just in getting the work done, but in understanding it.

The professor says stuff, and everyone already seems to know the answer. I never do.

Even worse than chemistry is calculus. It's just a bunch of senseless numbers. You're supposed to do things to them, and then come up with an answer that makes the teacher happy. I've been told that numbers are consistent, and comforting, and numbers never lie to you. That's bullshit. I never get the same answer twice, so they're not consistent. Which is not comforting. And numbers lie all the time. I know from statistics last semester. Numbers can be manipulated to justify anything you want.

Problem is, I need to pass these classes. I won't get into the pharmacy program if I can't get through calc and chem. I hate numbers. It's a good thing my mom is the business manager for the nursing home, so she does all the math that has to do with money. On the other hand, money math doesn't have integrals. There probably aren't a lot of fancy formulas for money. And nothing needs to be calculated past two decimal points. That would be a vast improvement.

A couple of my friends from biology dropped out of chemistry. I don't know if it was because it was too hard, or because of something else. Tiffany is trying to fit her class schedule around her work schedule, and they changed her hours at work, so she's in a different section. I have fewer people to help me, and that's bad, because I know I'm floundering.

At least I had an entire four-hour shift at the law library to try to get through my chemistry homework. I don't know if my answers are right or not, but at least I have something written down. It's awful when all I have to show for several hours is a few formulas that may or may not be right.

And, wouldn't you know it, in case life isn't bad enough, who should show up while I'm trying to wrap my brain around P orbitals, but Darcy Fitzwilliam.

"I'm sure whatever you're working on is very fascinating, but you're being paid to work at the circulation desk, not to sit and do personal work," his voice snapped at me.

I looked up. Yeah, Darcy all right. Who else would be that rude? I wanted to be really rude back, but I was determined I was going to one-up him. I would take the higher ground. "Terribly sorry, what can I get for you?"

He handed me a slip. "I need this from the restricted stacks. If it isn't too much trouble for you to do your job and go get it for me?"

I felt a delicious surge of power. He couldn't get it without my help. "Well, I'm happy to do my job, but it wouldn't hurt you to say 'please' or something else courteous."

He smiled tightly at me. "Would you go get me the goddamned book, please."

Naturally, that's when my boss walked up to us. "I'm sorry, sir, is there a problem?"

"No problem if she retrieves the book I'm asking for," he said, glaring at me.

My boss looked at me expectantly. "Well? What are you waiting for?"

I had no answer to that. I slid off my stool and went to get Darcy's book from the stacks. When I brought it back, I wanted to tell him he could choke on it, but of course, there was my boss, standing there, watching me. Now I was the bad guy with poor customer service skills. Just what I needed, Darcy getting me in trouble with my boss.

I asked for his library card, scanned it, scanned the book, and handed both over to him. "This is due back in two weeks."

Darcy took his stuff, turned on his heel, and left. My boss dropped a hand on my shoulder. "Why don't we go to my office."

Yeah, this was gonna be great. She closed the door, sat at her desk, and motioned for me to sit down. "Being rude to library patrons is not very professional."

"I wasn't being rude to him!" I protested. "He was being rude to me."

"This isn't going to be the last time a patron is rude to you. You are going to have to learn how to handle situations with tact and diplomacy. Provoking them until they swear at you isn't tact and diplomacy."

"I wasn't provoking him."

"Then what was the problem?"

I really resented the way she assumed I was the one who started it. But, at least I had an explanation that she should understand. "The problem is, we have a – history. He asked me out a little while ago, and I said no."

"Ah," she said, and nothing else.

I looked back at her for a moment, and when she didn't say anything else I figured that meant the ball was still in my court. "As you saw, he didn't take it very well."

She was pressing her lips together as she looked at me. I got the feeling she was trying hard not to laugh. Hoping I was right about that, I added, "I'm making you really, really glad you're not 18 anymore, aren't I?"

She passed a hand over her mouth. Yep, I'm sure she was wiping a smile off her face. "Well, you don't make it look like much fun, I will admit that."

"Can I get back to my post?" I asked.

"Go ahead," she answered.

"Thanks," I said, jumping out of my chair and heading back to the circulation desk. I swear I heard her giggle after I walked out of her office.

Feb 23

Tonight when I got back to my dorm room, I decided to declare my chemistry homework finished. I hadn't even touched my calculus homework. I got a start on it, but then Anne needed to get to bed. She said she didn't mind that I had my desk light on, but after an hour and I only got a couple of problems done, I thought I'd give up and go to sleep. I don't work well when I'm too tired, so it seemed like a pointless exercise. I might as well get some sleep.

That didn't work out, either. I couldn't sleep, all I could think about was that I'm going to flunk out of calculus and chemistry. And I hate Darcy Fitzwilliam. Well, I'll probably get a D in chemistry, it's the calculus that I'm really going to flunk.

Rather than lying in bed worrying about my unfinished calculus homework, and contemplating how irritating rich men's sons are, I figured I might as well go back to trying to get something done. I got up as quietly as I could, collected my stuff, and tiptoed out of the room.

I sat down on the couch in our little lounge and turned on the lamp, but I couldn't get settled. After about ten minutes of shifting this way and that, I decided to go downstairs to the common lounge instead. The big chairs in there are much more comfortable.

You would think the room would be empty at nearly 3:00 in the morning, but the lights were on, and there was someone sitting on the couch next to the big table.

It was Lon, the floor nerd. I've hardly seen him since the LAN party. Anne says he's in a whole lot of honors classes and I guess they keep those guys hopping.

"What are you doing up at this hour?" I asked, flopping down in the couch on the opposite side of the big table.

"Mechanical engineering project. What are you doing up?"

I wasn't going to tell him about Darcy, or about how stupid I am, and I can't make it through half my classes. I held up my calculus textbook. "If I can't sleep, I might as well get my homework done."

"Do you need any help?"

"If I do, do you mind?"

"Not at all." He didn't even look up from his laptop.

"Thanks." I pushed the cushions around so that I could be propped up on the couch with my book and notebook on my lap, and found my current assignment.

We both worked in a funny sort of silence. I would have said that it was a companionable silence, but it wasn't quite that comfortable. It was a little more tense than that.

I felt like he was looking at me, but if I looked at him out of the corner of my eye, I never caught him at it.

I got through the first half of my assignment, and then I came to a problem that I couldn't make heads or tails of. I really, really, didn't want to ask for his help. What's more awkward than getting help from a guy you won't go out with? But I was starting to get sleepy, and getting this done was more appealing than sitting there feeling like an idiot because I don't know how to do it myself. "Okay, I'm lost. Can I take you up on your offer to help?"

He looked up, and pushed his laptop aside. "What've you got?"

I brought him my textbook and sat next to him on his couch. "Here. Problem number ten. This sounds lame for someone who got a better grade in composition last semester than in any of my other classes, but I don't like word problems."

His lips twitched into something that was vaguely like a smile. He was always so serious looking. "All you're trying to do with word problems is glean the formula from the narrative. You should excel at that."

"You'd think. But I don't. I guess I'm a words person, not a numbers person."

He went through the problem with me, patiently explaining to me what the problem said in math terms.

"So all this is saying is figure out the rate of acceleration of the train?"

"Yep."

"You see why I don't like word problems."

"Would you like to do the next one, too?"

"If you don't mind."

"I wouldn't have offered if I minded."

I didn't know what to say to that. "Yeah. Sorry to make you state the obvious."

"Sometimes the obvious isn't so obvious when you're tired."

"It's nice of you to say so." I was feeling kind of squishy while he went through the explanation. After he explained the formula and what that problem was asking for, I really didn't want to ask him for any more help. "Okay, let me see if I can finish this now."

"All right."

I went back to my own couch, and he went back to his laptop. The last two were a little trickier, but eventually I realized that each of the problems was analogous to something the professor demonstrated in class. So I paired up the questions with his examples, like a multiple choice test. I got through the rest of the problems pretty quickly at that point. I closed my textbook with a tired sigh when I'd finished the last problem. "That's it. I'm done. And I think I can actually sleep now."

"Lucky you. I'll be up for a while yet. Good night."

"Thanks for your help. I appreciate it."

"Anytime."

Feb 24

I only sort of got my calculus homework right. Well, what do you expect for 3 o'clock in the morning? The ones Lon helped me with were right, of course, but a lot of the rest were pretty hit and miss. I am SO not a numbers girl.

So I lingered after class today to talk to the teacher. "Professor Jacobson? I don't suppose you've got a few minutes for a quick calculus for dummies lesson?"

He chuckled at my description. "I think the dummies don't pass the prerequisites for getting into calculus in the first place. But if you need some help, that's what my office hours are for."

"You don't mind if I come visit?"

"I like that better than you failing my class because you wouldn't come get help. That's why teachers have office hours, you know. So students can come ask for help."

"I don't need help. I need remedial math training." I sighed. "Although I think a different brain would help me a lot more. I don't suppose you keep spare brains in your office."

He scratched behind his ear. "Well, I usually keep a few in a jar on my desk, but I think it's empty at the moment."

"I'd say you can put mine in there, I'm not using it. On second thought, I am, just not for math problems. I'm a words person, not a numbers person."

"So you're the one that's going to be teaching engineers how to communicate someday," he said. I like him. He seems so compassionate. Like he really understands people. Seems kind of odd for a math professor. You'd think math professors would be the sort who dealt in numbers because they don't know how to deal with people.

"That would be sort of ideal, now that you mention it," I said. "So when are your office hours?"

Students were starting to enter the classroom for the next class. "It's on page one of your syllabus, along with the room number," he answered. "I do apologize, I have to get to my next class. Come see me during office hours."

He set off at a brisk pace. I watched him walk away. He's tall, and lean, and has great hair for a guy old enough to be my father. Come to think of it, there isn't much fatherly about him.

I thought about him a lot while I walked over to the student union. Marianne Dashwood wasted her time on a stupid boy her own age before she figured out that the best man for her was about 20 years older than her. Maybe I need to follow her example. Better yet, I can improve upon her example. Colonel Brandon had to patiently wait forever for Marianne to figure things out and grow up. If a Colonel Brandon liked me, I wouldn't be so silly as to avoid him. A virile older man would be a big improvement over the jerk I'd been putting up with last semester.

Feb 26

I blew off my coffee date with Allie and her mom, and went to Professor Jacobson's office this afternoon, right after Spanish class. He really is helping me get a better idea of what I'm doing. At least I could get the right answers for the problems on the homework assignment that I'd failed. I think that's all I've ever done in math classes. Just give them what they want. If you do things with numbers until they're happy, that's all that's required. The trick is doing the right things and giving them the numbers they want. That part isn't always easy.

Just as we finished, and I was putting my book back in my book bag, my cell phone tweeted that I had a text message. "I'm sorry, I thought I'd put this thing on vibrate," I apologized. "Let me put it on silent so that it doesn't keep making noises at me." When I picked up my phone, I saw it was Anne. It said "Phil says you told Darcy that he's an asshole? Are you out of your mind? Do you know how much he's worth?"

I threw my phone into my purse. That was weeks ago. I mean, really, can't I get on with my life by now? Now I knew I was right not to tell Anne anything about the whole Darcy debacle in the first place. She's a sorority girl, and more materialistic than I am. I guess that makes her my Charlotte Lucas, if I'm still living out my own private *Pride and Prejudice*. I frowned at the thought. I don't want to be living *P&P* anymore. It isn't as much fun in real life as it was on paper, and it's just not turning out the same way.

"Trouble?" Professor Jacobson asked me. That's when I realized I'd made a disgusted noise when I'd seen the text. And when I threw the phone in my bag.

"Yeah. I'd summarize that it's boy trouble, but that's too simplistic. I just – I'm no good at the dating thing."

He eyed me with a gentle smile that made me forget Darcy, and Anne, and Jane Austen. "I don't think anyone is good at the dating thing. It's scary, and full of pitfalls, and everyone is terrified of making mistakes."

"If that's true, why does everyone seem to make so many mistakes? You'd think if people were so worried about making mistakes, they'd be trying extra hard not to."

"It's not simply about intentions. It's like calculus – you have to find the right formula. If you have the wrong formula, you're not going to get the results you're looking for."

I looked at him for a couple moments, processing what he'd said. "I'd never thought of math as a metaphor for mating rituals before."

"Well, let's say you're trying to cheer up a boyfriend. If it's a new boyfriend, you don't know what makes him happy. It could be football, or basketball, or it could be D&D. Maybe he likes Mexican food. Maybe he hates Mexican food. If he calls you and says he's having a bad day, you don't know if the thing to do is wear a sweatshirt with his favorite sports team, or take him out for a beer, or go jogging.

"Now, let's say you've had one boyfriend for a while. You get to know his likes and dislikes. You know how to cheer him up, and how to irritate him. Then you break up with him and get a new boyfriend. If you use the same formula on a new boyfriend that you did on the old boyfriend, you're not going to get the same results. Boyfriend One loved the Packers, and you could cheer him up by wearing a Packers shirt. But Boyfriend Two doesn't even like football. So wearing a Packers shirt isn't going to help much. If Boyfriend Two loves the Beatles, and going to Renaissance Festivals, you can cheer him up by singing 'All You Need is Love,' and suggesting you could go to the Ren Faire this weekend.

"You have to get the formula right. Once you understand what the formula is, everything else becomes much easier."

"That's great, but how do you figure out what the formula is? That's the part that seems to be giving me trouble," I slumped back in my chair.

"It's all trial and error. Ask a lot of questions. That's what a first date is for. Finding out if there's any connection between you that's worth exploring on a second date."

"You make it sound so simple and scientific."

He toyed with his pencil, and I couldn't take my eyes off his hands. He has really nice hands. They look strong, but gentle. "It is, in a way. It seems complicated, because there's so much organic chemistry involved. Everyone knows that organic chemistry is hopelessly complicated and best left to the experts. We're living organisms, and we're subject to it. You aptly referred to the process as 'mating rituals.' Every species on the planet has its own set of rules. And there isn't a species out there that has decided 'Never mind, this is too complicated' and gives up."

"Well, maybe there was, but that species would die out in a single generation," I answered.

He nodded. "That's right. And humans have had a long time to come up with rules, then societies spring up and impose different codes on top of that."

"What do you mean?"

"Well, most current religions of the world have a lot of rules about repressing and controlling sexuality. Forbidding homosexuality, for example. Which, you'll notice still happens, despite society making rules to forbid it. The ancient Greeks had a thoroughly bisexual culture. Instead of forbidding it, it was expected. A young man would have been initiated into sex by an older man. But then at some point in time he would be expected to take a wife, and reproduce. And then some day he would be the older man who takes a young male lover."

"That's wild," I said. I hoped he would keep talking. It seemed very promising that he was talking to me about sex, even if he was doing it in this very academic way.

"The current patriarchal religions of the world enforce monogamy, and forbid any sex outside of marriage. I think they're starting to give up on that idea. People have sex before they get married, and churches are having to accept that. People have extramarital affairs, even though that's forbidden, too. It would be simpler to obey the rules, but people don't. It may be complicated, but people do it. We're clearly not a monogamous species.

"Society wasn't always into monogamy. Even Christianity wasn't. The Bible is filled with men who had several wives. Society's rules on what was sexually acceptable were very different.

"So, this has turned into a lecture, and I apologize, but I'm just saying that between the demands of your hormones, the reproductive urges that every species on the planet is subject to, and the rules and expectations of society, of course dating is difficult and confusing."

He smiled at me, warmly, sympathetically, and my legs turned to goo. I was glad I was still sitting. "You do have a way of making it all seem less complicated. Or at least less frustrating. Both calculus and life. Thank you, Professor Jacobson."

He smiled at me again as I stood up, making me sorry I'd stood up at that particular moment. "You're welcome. Feel free to drop in again if you need more help."

"I will." He invited me back, I will have to accept his invitation!

Feb 28

I've been thinking about my conversation with Professor Jacobson over and over. The thing about formulas and people. It seems both complicated and simple at the same time. I'm trying to decide if it's also a very unromantic way of looking at the world. It makes a certain kind of sense, but does it lack a romantic sensibility?

Ha! *Sense and Sensibility*!

This is the second time that Professor Jacobson has me thinking about *S&S*. Well, if I'm no Lizzie Bennett, there are worse things in life than being a Marianne Dashwood. She had youth and beauty and high spirits. She wasn't good at the dating thing, either, and overlooked the better man at first. Why was that? Did Colonel Brandon seem unromantic at first impression?

Even though I've got an assignment due in Spanish, as well as the inevitable calc and chem homework, I grabbed *Sense and Sensibility* to take with me to read while I went to dinner. I wanted to read everything in the book about Colonel Brandon.

Anne spotted me in the dining hall while I was halfway through a tuna sandwich and a really big pile of potato chips. "Hey, Roomie." Without waiting for an invitation, she slid her cafeteria tray onto the table across from me and plopped her book bag down beside it.

"Hey, yourself," I managed to say around a mouthful of potato chip, then swallowed. "I can't remember, when was the last time I saw you in public without a sorority sister or two with you? What happened, did they kick you out?"

"I do have some life outside of Greek life," she said. Then she looked at the book in my hand. "You having a really bad day?"

"Um, no I don't think so, why?" I asked.

"Usually, if you're having a bad day, you pick up Jane Austen and read a little something before you start to study. Since instead of sitting here doing your homework, you're sitting here reading Jane Austen, I take it you had an exceptionally bad day today."

"Wow, I didn't know I did that," I laughed. "I don't think today was particularly bad. I was thinking about a conversation I've had recently, and I wanted to compare it to something I read in here."

"Just as long as you're not comparing some real-life guy to the romantic hero of a romance novel," she looked at me skeptically.

"What's wrong with romantic heroes?" I asked.

"It's not real life. Darcy Fitzwilliam asks you out, and you turn him down because he's not the Mr. Darcy of your romance novel."

"I turned him down because he was an asshole to me," I corrected her.

"Well, guys can be assholes sometimes. You shouldn't pass judgment on them until you know them better."

I smiled at her. "Actually, that's exactly the point of *Pride and Prejudice*."

She gave me a doubtful look. "My point is that life isn't like a romance novel. Get your nose out of your books and live a real romance, instead of trying to make your life resemble somebody else's made-up one."

"A lot of people go through life without anything romantic ever happening to them at all. They don't know where to look. If Jane's novels help me figure out where to look, what's wrong with that?"

"It's not real life," she insisted. "That's why they call it fiction."

"Good fiction is based on universal truths," I countered.

"It's still not real. And besides, you should be working on your chemistry and calculus assignments, not sitting here reading a book that you probably know by heart."

I put the book down. "Yes, you've got the right of me on that one."

"I what?" she laughed at me. "Is that some English expression from one of her books?"

"Maybe, I don't know. I just thought it sounded cooler than saying, 'Yeah, you're right.' "

"Have you ever thought about being an English major instead of a pharmacy major?" she asked me.

"I don't want to be an English major. There are no jobs for English majors after they get out of college," I answered contemptuously.

"But you could teach classes on Jane Austen," she pointed out.

"I'm no good at public speaking. I sort of freeze up," I admitted.

"There's just no hope for you, is there?" she laughed.

"I guess not," I agreed with her.

Feb 29

Colonel Brandon is really not quite the same as Professor Jacobson. Colonel Brandon is a man of few words: Professor Jacobson doesn't mind talking. But both of them are kind, and considerate, and like to be helpful to others. So for the most part, they're very similar.

When I turned in my next calculus assignment, I only got it about half right. Unfortunately, I didn't know until the next assignment was due which part was less than half right. So, when I got them back, I figured it was time to take him up on that invitation to visit him again during his office hours. He said if I needed more help, I should come back. Well, considering my success rate (or is that a lack-of-success rate?), I think this qualifies as needing more help.

I love his office. This is probably a really stupid way to describe it, but his office is so...academic. There are lots of shelves full of books and papers, and there are books stacked up on the window ledge, and piles of papers stacked on his desk. He's also got a little corner with a table and a couple of chairs, and a cabinet with an electric kettle and a tea pot and a few boxes of different teas sitting on top of it. Even the fact that he's a tea drinker, not a coffee drinker, seems so academic. All he needs is a British accent to be complete, somehow. I don't know why he would seem even more scholarly with a British accent, but he would.

He was on the phone when I popped my head in his door. He waved me in while he kept talking. "That's fine. It really doesn't matter if you want to send me the final draft in installments, instead of all at once. I can only read one page at a time, after all." He smiled at me and shrugged his shoulders a little, as if to say 'You know what I mean?' I smiled and shrugged back at him. The next thing he said made no sense to me. "Well, yeah. Mint chocolate chip." He chuckled. "That's why you like writing books with me. I keep you entertained. Right. Talk to you later." He hung up, and turned his attention to me. "Sorry about that."

"I'm the one that's sorry to interrupt," I said, then turned to a more interesting topic than pleasantries. "You've written a book?"

"It's hard to get tenure if you don't publish. Yes, I've written a few books." He pointed to one of the shelves. I walked over to take a look. There it was! His name was on the covers. He'd written something like 8 or 10 books.

"That's amazing!" I exclaimed. "That's why you're able to teach, you can explain things well enough to write about them."

He looked amused. "You hadn't noticed, then, I take it."

"Noticed what?" I asked.

He pointed to the cover of my textbook for his class. I had put it down on his desk while I looked at his bookshelf. There was his name, along with another name. No doubt the person he just got off the phone with.

"So you write all the math problems I have to solve."

"Actually, my partner tends to write the problems, I mostly write the explanations of the concepts."

I suddenly remembered his odd non sequitur. "What does mint chocolate chip have to do with writing math textbooks?"

"It's an ice cream flavor." He offered no other explanation. I could tell he was being mysterious just to keep me curious.

"What does ice cream have to do with math?" I didn't mind asking.

"My partner was calling me a smart ass. You know what a smart ass is, right? It's someone who can sit on a gallon of ice cream and tell you what flavor it is."

I just looked at him. I wasn't sure how to respond to that. It was obviously some kind of in-joke between them.

He looked back at me. "It's kind of like a joke, but smaller."

I nodded, and then figured it was time to get to the reason I came to see him. Well, just coming to see him was reason enough, but I still had the problem of these failed assignments. I pulled the pages out from where I'd crammed them inside my textbook. "I don't suppose you can go over our last two assignments with me? I kind of bombed them."

He held out his hand. "Let's take a look, shall we? And while we're at it, would you like a cup of tea? I just made a fresh pot. Cups are in the cabinet, and sugar is in the peanut butter jar."

I poured myself some tea, and looked over his tea selection while he pulled a chair over so I could sit next to him while he went over my assignments.

I'm not sure how much information I absorbed, but it was still a pleasant hour, sitting with him, having tea, his pleasant voice explaining what I had done wrong, and what I should have done instead. I was sitting so close to him, I also couldn't help but notice he smells like leather and clean linen.

March 14

Tea and calculus. It's becoming a thing. I've started drinking tea while I do my calculus homework, just to channel my time in Professor Jacobson's office, and he has tea waiting for me when I come in for his office hours. He has office hours twice a week, we have class three times a week. So I have to fly on my own some of the time, but most of the time I'm able to bring in my completed assignments before I turn them in, and have him check them over.

"Making us do trigonometry and integrals at the same time is not nice," I told him when I walked in. "You are not a kind person."

"The water is ready in the electric kettle, why don't you pick the tea and make us a pot? Everything looks better with a cup of tea," he directed me.

I sorted through his collection. "Earl Grey, Lapsang Souchong, Assam, English Breakfast, Irish Breakfast, Keemun, Golden Yunnan. You really love your black teas. Do you have any Russian Caravan in this collection?"

His forehead wrinkled a little between his eyebrows. "I've never heard of it."

"Oh, you'd love it. It's delicious." I picked the Irish Breakfast, and poured in the steaming hot water.

"I will have to try it sometime." There was a companionable silence while I got out two cups and the sugar while he looked over the page I'd handed him.

"You're right, numbers are not your friend," he said with a smile when I handed him his cup.

"Someone in class said he loved numbers, because numbers never lie. That's totally not true. Numbers lie to me all the time," I moaned. He laughed at me, then looked thoughtful.

"If I gave you one of these questions and asked you to do it again, would you get the same result? Or would you get a different answer every time?"

"I don't know," I answered. "I don't usually do the same problems over and over again."

"Well, why don't you try that?" he suggested. "Some of the time, you get the answer right. Then you do another problem using the same principle, but you get the answer wrong. You know how to do it, but you aren't doing it consistently."

The idea of taking two or three times as long to get my homework done was horrifying. But I didn't want him thinking I'm lazy. He knows I'm stupid; I need to have some redeeming qualities. "I can try that."

"When you get the same answer twice in a row, then you've probably got it right," he said. "Give that a try. You're making progress, you really are."

"It's slow and stupid progress, but it's progress," I shrugged.

"Well, any sort of progress is a good thing. Take your successes as they come, and be happy about it." He was writing as we talked, now he pushed a fresh sheet of paper with a calc problem on it at me. "Now, do this problem, and explain the process to me out loud while you do it."

"Did I get this one wrong, or right on my homework?" I asked.

He smiled gently. "I'll tell you after you finish answering it."

March 21

Yes, Professor Jacobson is about the kindest, most gallant man in the whole universe!

I have my parents' car for the week. They all took spring break to go to Arizona to visit my grandparents. It's totally not fair. David and Wendy have their spring break a different week than I do. Grandma's not doing too well, but I couldn't skip school for ten days in order to go with them. With the way I'm struggling in chemistry and calculus, I can't exactly skip classes. So off they went, and I have to stay behind.

When they drove in to fly out of the airport, they picked me up on the way, and my consolation prize for not seeing Grandma and Grandpa is that I get to have the car for a week.

I'm totally having fun with it. Anne and I ran out to get an electric kettle and an air popcorn popper for our room. I picked up Ken from Spanish class on Tuesday evening, and we went to dinner at a Mexican place off campus. It's really off the beaten path; there are no bus lines or anything that go nearby. If you don't have a car, you don't go there. Then Wednesday I met Allie and her mom at the thrift store.

I guess I've gone hog wild on the driving around thing; today I missed calculus because I was still driving back to school!

I thought I had enough time to run out and try and get my phone fixed. It needs to charge more and more often, and I wanted to see if there is something they can do. Replace the battery or something. I was wrong. It's a longer trip out and back than I realized. Driving takes time. Salesmen who want me to buy an expensive new phone take even more time.

I was frantic. Professor Jacobson would notice that I wasn't there. He knows I'm barely staying on top of assignments, how was I going to manage after I'd missed the lecture? What would he think of me? I pushed the speed limit as much as I dared, hoping maybe I could catch the end of the lecture.

When it started raining and traffic slowed to a crawl, I started crying with frustration.

And then, as I was turning onto the campus, I got a flat tire.

That's when I started crying harder.

I heard there is some sort of car club that people belong to, so if you have problems with your car, you call them and they come to help. I'm going to get myself one of these memberships. I don't know the first thing about how to deal with a flat tire. Okay, that's not true. I know what to do in theory, but I've never touched a tire iron before. Or used a jack.

I waited for a little while for it to stop raining. No such luck. It was really coming down. I could tell it was going to keep doing this all day, so I might as well deal with it. I was gonna get wet.

I pulled up my collar against the rain, for all the good it was going to do me, and ran around to open the trunk and start finding stuff.

It was a cold rain. The temperature must have dropped fifteen degrees when it started pouring. I whimpered as it hit me, and I made a mental note to get my parents an umbrella next Christmas that could live in the car all the time. I lifted the trunk panel, pulled out the little emergency spare, and the tire iron, and the funny little jack thing. I knelt down by the flat tire, which was on the rear driver's side, and got splashed by a car driving past.

Asshole. I was swearing and crying at the same time. I had to kneel in the wet street, in my boots and miniskirt, giving the drivers a show while I tried to get the jack in place. I actually did it, and putting the tire iron in the slot gave me the leverage I needed to lift the car.

When I started trying to loosen the bolts on the tire, I discovered that you're supposed to do that step before you lift up the car. The wheel would turn, and I couldn't push. I had to figure out how to switch the jack so I could lower the car again. By now I was soaked to the skin, freezing cold, and hating my life pretty thoroughly. I took the tire iron off the jack, and flipped it around to use on the bolts. I think they're called lug nuts, which wouldn't be bolts at all...

That's when I discovered I couldn't budge them at all. I don't know if it was because the tire iron was so wet and slippery, or because I don't have very strong hands, or because I was doing it wrong. I know it's righty-tighty, lefty-loosey, but maybe I had the perspective wrong. I tried the next nut. Wouldn't budge. I tried another. Nope. I started crying again in frustration.

That's when I heard a voice shouting my name. I stood up and looked around to see who was calling to me.

It was Professor Jacobson! He was in his car, leaving campus, in the lane closer to me. "Lizzie! Hang tight, I'll come give you a hand."

I stood there, shivering, wiping the tears off my face, which was pointless, my entire head was soaked from the rain. Which of course included my face.

Professor Jacobson pulled up behind me, turned on his flashers, and dashed out. "Can't get them to budge?" he asked.

"No," I answered. "Which is making me wish I'd paid more attention in physics class last year. I'm sure there's a formula for how to do this, how much force to use, how long of a lever, and stuff."

"You're starting to think like a mathematician, I'm proud of you," I could tell he was amused by me. I would have been glad of it if I wasn't so wet. "Go sit in my car, I'll take care of this for you."

I pushed wet hair out of my eyes. I felt like a drowned rat. Talk about not a moment for impressing men. "Thank you," I wasn't about to argue with him.

He must have been planning ahead, he had his heater turned on full blast when I got inside. Sitting on the passenger side, I could only sort of see him working on my tire. He made quick work of it, or at least a lot faster than I had been doing things. It still seemed to take forever in the rain.

But, he wasn't completely soaked through when he put the flat tire in my parents' trunk, and ran back to get in his car.

"You're set for now, don't drive too quickly or too far. Those spares are designed to get you to the nearest mechanic."

"My dorm is only a few minutes from here," I assured him.

"That's good." He watched me shivering and dripping. "You should get home and get dry. A hot shower is probably in order, if you can stand the thought of any more water right now." He smiled that smile of his which always made me go all weak and squishy.

"I can do that."

"Good girl. Is your mechanic nearby?"

"I don't know; it's my parents' car. I've got use of it for the week."

"I'll give you the name of a guy I go to. He's only a few blocks from here. He's dependable, and not too expensive."

"Thank you."

He squeezed my shoulder with his hand. "Now, get home and out of those wet clothes as fast as you can."

I smiled, nodded, and opened the car door. I ran as fast as I could to my car and got in. I could see he was going to wait for me to go first, so I waved at him in the rear view mirror and took off.

It was only when I was parked and running from the lot to my dorm that I realized that him telling me to get out of my wet clothes could have more than one meaning. I checked the mirror in the bathroom before I got in the shower stall and started peeling off my soaking things. My shirt was a little bit transparent as it clung to me. And it wasn't hard to see that my bra was a leopard print.

It wasn't quite as romantic as the movie when Colonel Brandon goes riding out in the rain looking for Marianne, but it was sort of close. And, in a way, perhaps a bit sexier in the end.

April 14

Well, I will never be a genius at calculus, but at least I should get a passing grade in the class. At least Professor Jacobson thinks I'm putting in a heroic effort. He said so, straight out, today when I went to see him.

"You are a truly courageous person," he told me.

I brightened at his compliment, even though I didn't understand it. "Why do you say that I'm courageous?"

"Well, you don't see math majors taking linguistics courses, do you? Or engineers taking writing classes. But even though you know this is a struggle for you, here you are stubbornly determined to conquer calculus. That's pretty good for a – what are you, Spanish major, was it?"

I'm so pleased that he puts such a positive spin on my frequent visits. And I didn't want to tell him that I'm supposed to be going into pharmacology. He'd just look at me with pity and horror, so I didn't bother to correct him. "You have such a kind way of saying things. Anyone else would have given up and admitted that I'm stupid at math."

"You're definitely not stupid."

"But I'm stupid with numbers. You even agreed they're not my friends. You pointed out how all people have their strengths and weaknesses. No one's good at everything, and if there was such a person, we either have to kill that person for being insufferable, or we have to make that person breed copiously, to strengthen the species."

"That reminds me," Professor Jacobson said, digging in one of his desk drawers. "I realized I had a spare copy of something I

thought you'd enjoy." He pulled a book out of the drawer, and slid it across to me.

I picked it up. The cover said *The Naked Ape*. He's given me a book with the word naked in the title. I wonder if it's a message!

"Since we had that conversation about mating rituals the first time you came to see me, I thought you'd enjoy this. It's a classic book on human behavior. Desmond Morris is a zoologist, he studied people and primate behavior the same way he studied cats and dogs. He's written any number of books explaining what people do and why."

I scooped the book up. "Thanks! This sounds awesome!" I reached for my book bag. "I have something for you, too, but it isn't nearly so cerebral. Since you drink tea, but you hadn't heard of Russian Caravan, I brought you some." I handed him a box of teabags, and a little jar of honey. "Since you prefer your tea sweetened, you really want this one sweetened with honey. It's fantastic with honey."

"Well, we should make a pot, then, shouldn't we!" He popped up from his desk chair, and went over to get his electric kettle. "Fortunately, I haven't made any tea yet. We can try it out while we go over your homework."

I moved my books over to the table and got out the assignment, my guts absolutely squishy with excitement. He liked my gift. And he had one for me, too!

We had our usual tea and integrals together. I did a lot better on my homework, since I'm taking his advice and doing problems multiple times until I get matching answers. "You're definitely improving," he nodded as he showed me where I went wrong on one of my problems.

"Thanks to your patience," I was sitting next to him, so I nudged him affectionately with my shoulder.

"I never mind helping students who honestly try their best," he said.

"It's never going to come easy to me, though. I assume most math majors find this all incredibly simple."

"Mostly," he admitted. "And they're probably getting remedial lessons in their English classes, since they're numbers people, not words people." He gave my own expression back to me.

"Are math majors as bad as engineers?" I asked.

"Maybe not as bad." He thought about it a moment, then smiled. "But we all have our areas where we are doomed to fail. I won't tell you what sort of grades I got in my history classes when I was an undergrad."

"Were you really horrible?" I asked, trying to imagine what he looked like at 18 or 19 years old, taking history and English 101 and whatever else was considered basic gen ed when he was in my shoes.

He looked at me. I think he was trying to decide how much to tell me. "Yeah, I was pretty awful. I'm actually kind of a slow reader, and they give you huge reading assignments, and expect you to memorize endless numbers of dates. I don't memorize well."

"You must have to memorize all these formulas," I pointed out.

"Sure, but if I can't remember it, I can always extrapolate it. You can't extrapolate dates. Christopher Columbus set sail on one specific date in history. Saying he set sail in October, when in truth it was June, is the wrong answer. And how are you supposed to figure it out? There's no formula for figuring it out. You just have to know. It's like spelling. There's one right way to spell a word, you can't extrapolate how something is spelled."

"Well, you can a little bit, if you know what language a word comes from. Bureau is French, so you get that E-A-U combination, instead of a nice, simple letter O. Cafeteria is Spanish, so you spell it pretty much exactly as it sounds. Karaoke we get from Japanese, that's why it ends in O-K-E. Egg comes from Old Norse, that's why it has two g's. Aardvark has two a's in it because it's Dutch."

He was looking at me in amazement. "Wow! You really are a words person."

"I like words." I also liked the way he was looking at me. Like I was smart. And I just showed him there was more to me than the stupid girl who can't do calculus or fix a flat tire without a whole lot of extra help.

"Well, that's probably why you're a Spanish major. It suits you. I'm sure you'll be fabulous as a translator. You're personable, and if numbers aren't your friends, words are."

I looked down at my Spanish book, sitting there under the calculus textbook. I really should tell him the truth, but it was so nice to have him tell me I'll be fabulous at something.

I wanted to stay there all afternoon, but I had to get to chem lab right about the time his office hours were over. I walked across campus with the biggest smile on my face. Even though I'm a math moron, he thinks I'm clever.

May 20

The time between spring break and finals has absolutely flown by. I've tried asking for more help in chemistry, which I should have done much earlier. But if I'm honest, I must say I just don't like it all that much. I've already established that numbers are not my friend, and there are an awful lot of numbers in chemistry. I have trouble caring what Avogadro's Number is. Numbers are bad enough when they're simple. Any number that ends in the letter e is not really a number. And why would you use an e if the number means the same thing every time? I asked my TA about that, he just scowled at me. He also didn't like it when he overheard me in the lab, saying that chemistry is just like cooking, except you don't get something fun when you're done. Just a beaker full of smelly chemicals.

At least calculus, while it doesn't make much more sense to me than chemistry, when I ask for help, I don't get looked at like I'm an idiot. Instead, a guy who is easy on the eyes and has a nice smile gives me encouragement and says I'm not as stupid as I think I am, and says "Wow" when I list off the root languages of English words.

After final exams, I managed to find out my grades before my dad came to pick me up to go home for the summer. I'm not too surprised that my chemistry grade is pretty bad. But I got a B- in calculus!

I was so excited, I had to go see Professor Jacobson. I had no idea if he would be in his office. Professors only have to give exams, and they don't have to pack up their dorm rooms, so they probably post their grades from home and don't bother to come in. But I had to try. Maybe there's other stuff they have to do, like extra paperwork or something.

I nearly ran down the hall when I saw the light in the hallway coming from his office door. I hoped it wasn't just the cleaning staff, if colleges have cleaning staffs.

There he was! I bounced into his office with a big smile on my face. "Did you see? Did you see?" I jumped up and down while

I asked, which was making my pigtails swing wildly. I realized after I started bouncing that I was wearing a shirt that's kind of tight, so other things were probably bouncing up and down, too.

He turned around from where he was taking something off one of his shelves and smiled, like he always does. "What's that?" he asked.

"You gave me a B minus! I passed your class!" I told him, and proceeded to do a happy dance while he looked at me in amusement.

"Of course I saw, I'm the one who gave you the grade. You earned it," he said with that warmth that always made me love being in the same room with him. "See, you're a lot better math student than you thought."

"I have you to thank for it, you're awesome!" I squealed. I threw my arms around his neck, and kissed him.

I could feel his body stiffen against mine. I realized he wasn't kissing back, though my aim had been right on the money.

He pulled his face back away from mine, and his hands reached up to unclasp mine from around his neck. Then he stepped away from me.

"Did I do something wrong?" I asked.

"Well, not quite. I'm glad you're excited about your grade, but there are rules about how much a professor may fraternize with a student. Especially a female student. That kind of crossed a line. If anyone had seen that, I'd be having to explain myself, or else lose my job."

"Oh. But, I..." I spluttered a little.

"Don't be embarrassed. I know you were just excited." He went over and sat at his desk. I stood in front of him, looking down at him uncertainly.

"I am, but…" I didn't know how to ask him. "I also kind of thought that maybe you liked me."

"I do like you," he answered, then his expression changed. "Oh. You mean, like, like you." He scrutinized me a bit, while I could feel my face turning red. "I'm sorry, I didn't realize that's what you were thinking. I'm old enough to be your father."

I could hear Marianne Dashwood protesting "But he's so old!" in the back of my head. "Are you sure?"

"You must be what, eighteen?" he asked me.

"Nineteen," I corrected him.

"I have a son who is nineteen. I'd love to introduce you to him, but he's studying abroad in Germany right now. I think the two of you would hit it off."

"You want to set me up with your son?" I asked miserably. "That's why you've been so nice to me?"

He sat forward to put his chin on his hand, which partially covered his mouth. I wondered for a moment if he was trying not to laugh. "No, actually it hadn't occurred to me until now," he answered. "Are you not used to your teachers being nice to you?"

"I, no, but I was thinking maybe…" I could tell my face was turning redder, and redder, and redder.

"I see. Well, you are a delightful young lady, Lizzie, and I am very flattered. I'm sorry if any of my conduct made you believe I had a romantic interest in you. But I really do like my job, and I would very much like to keep it. I'd also like to keep my wife, and I think she might take a dim view of having young competition."

"Oh." I stood there, at a loss as to what to say. I wanted to run out of the room, but I didn't want to be melodramatic. Since I had no dignity left whatsoever, running away seemed like the worst thing I could do. "I'm sorry for the misunderstanding. I hope I didn't embarrass you."

"Not much. Maybe just a little. As I said, I'm flattered." He smiled at me, that same warm smile he always has for me, which makes my stomach do flip flops. It was the same smile that made me think he'd been interested in me...

"Well, I'll get out of your hair. I came over to thank you for all your help this semester before my dad comes to take me home," I started backing up toward the door and sort of waved at him.

"Congratulations," he said.

I walked out of his office, knowing I could never set foot in there ever again. Since his door was open, I had to walk casually down the hall, because I knew he'd be able to hear my footsteps.

Once I got down the stairs and out of the building, I was able to run away as fast as my legs could take me.

I was happy that the campus was mostly deserted. I wasn't fit to be seen in public. I cried as I ran, desperately wanting to hide in my room. Even if it's only my room for a couple more hours. At least that was one way I could be like Marianne. I know how to give vent to my feelings. I hope my father doesn't show up too soon. I need some quality time with my pillow. So much for my Colonel Brandon! I have just made a complete fool of myself.

While it's bad my father is coming soon, I realize as I sit here, sobbing and writing, that it's also a good thing. I'm going home where I am not going to have to look at anything related to college for a few months. No daily reminders of Professor Jacobson. I'm going to be drinking more coffee from now on, since tea will always make me think of him.

May 30

Well, this summer already sucks.

My parents are not pleased with my grades. I got an A in western philosophy and Spanish, which they consider irrelevant. They frowned, but didn't have much to say about the B- in calculus, thankfully. I won't think about calculus ever again. Even the word makes me blush with mortification. For that matter, so does tea. I hid the book he gave me, *The Naked Ape*, at the back of one of my bookshelves. I can't bring myself to throw it out, since it's the only present he ever gave me. But I don't want to see it, either. And I'm never going to be able to read it.

But my F in chemistry and chem lab is making for a whole lot of unhappiness. I got accused of everything under the sun; doing drugs, partying too much, secret boyfriends, and just plain laziness. They are furious with me. I'm their daughter, and my poor grades hurt their pride. My mother even called the professor to get an explanation. (Talk about a whole new kind of humiliation!)

My father got me a summer job at our local Walgreens, where I can learn more about the pharmacy "biz." I hate it. I'm an assistant to the assistants to the pharmacist. I find all these small bottles and labels and little paper bags totally tedious. I stock the shelves with all the pills that come in from the pharmaceutical companies, and that's also tedious. If this is what my father wants me to learn, that pharmacy is a tedious business, and I hate it, well, I've learned that lesson really well.

June 16

So, here's another lesson to go with how much I hate the drug "biz:" don't make any mistakes, or you'll get fired.

Yesterday we got in two shipments of pills from two different companies. All of them come in small white boxes that look pretty much the same. Sometimes the names look a lot alike, too. Problem is, Levoxyl (also called Levothyroxine) and Levofloxacin (also known as Levaquin) are not the same thing. One is for something to do with the thyroid, and the other is an antibiotic.

Unfortunately, when you get them mixed up, you get in a whole lot of trouble.

Fortunately, they discovered my mixup before anyone got the wrong drug, which would not only be bad, but also potentially fatal. Even thought they caught my mistake in time, I still got fired.

My parents have gone ballistic. They can't believe I made such a stupid mistake, and I embarrassed them with the pharmacist at Walgreens, who was a personal friend willing to hire me in the first place.

So then I got to tell them I'm just not pharmacist material.

It was a pretty ugly conversation. How could I possibly not want to do what they wanted me to do? They've been telling me most of my life that I'm going to be a pharmacist for their nursing home. Since I always got perfectly good grades in high school, I must be doing something wrong. Maybe I need to come back and go to the community college here in town, where they can keep a closer eye on me.

"I'm living here at home where you can keep an eye on me, but I still lost my job with the pharmacy," I pointed out. "Why don't you just face it, I'm no good at this stuff. I don't like it, it bores me. I don't like chemistry, I don't like math, it's not a good fit for me. I'll probably never be able to get into a pharmacy program. If I can't get through the prerequisites, how am I going to get through the rest of the classes?

"Well, then, what do you plan to do with the rest of your life?" my father demanded to know.

"I don't know yet, but let me at least go back to school and work on my gen ed requirements, so I'm still working towards a degree of some kind or another." I thought maybe I had them, there. "You still want me to get a college degree, right? You don't want me to drop out of college if I'm not getting the degree you want me to get?"

"The degree is still important," my father admitted. "But maybe you should come home and take a few classes here in town until you figure out what you want to do."

I didn't want to come home. "A big part of my schooling is being paid for with grants and scholarships and loans," I pointed out. "I will lose that if I don't go back this fall."

"Aren't they tied to you going into pharmacy?" Mom asked.

"No, they're tied to my good grades in high school," I pointed out. "They didn't know or care what I was going to major in when they gave me the money. They just thought I was a good investment in the future. I'm not going to be a good investment if I keep trying to do something I hate."

"You really hate chemistry?"

"I hated chemistry, and biology, and calculus," I answered honestly. Of course I started blushing the moment I said the last word. "I am not going to make a good scientist. I need to go find something that I'm actually going to be good at. Poisoning the patients at your facility will get you sued, and then you'll lose the whole business because of me. Maybe Wendy or David will make a good pharmacist. You do have three kids, after all, not just me. "

"I guess that's fair," my father said. I was so relieved that they stopped yelling at me, it only later occurred to me that now I have to figure out what I really am going to do with my life.

SOPHOMORE YEAR

Aug 25

I thought this summer was never going to end! I ended up working at McDonald's, which my parents hated, but I enjoyed. I wasn't under pressure from all kinds of wild expectations. I just had to take orders at the drive up window and handle money and make change. And assemble cheeseburgers. And scoop fries – no one cares about exactly how many fries are in a carton. It made me feel like the All-American teenager. Like Allie's mom says, what is more American than McDonald's?

I've registered for NO science or math courses this semester. I decided that, since I really liked the philosophy class I took last spring, I'll try following up on that. Maybe I can be a philosophy major. There is such a thing. What does one do with a philosophy degree? That's probably one of the ways of being pre-law. I don't know if I want to be a lawyer, since after all Darcy is in law school. But it would be silly of me to avoid a career path just because of one rich jackass.

It turns out, my best friend since 6th grade is taking me back to school! Eddie Jameson was away most of the summer serving as a ranger with the National Park Service. How cool is that? It was the perfect job for him. He's great at rock climbing, and crawling in caves, and anything else that involves the outdoors. He's also sort of the quiet type. We both didn't like having to give presentations in front of our classes in school. But he says it wasn't so bad dealing with people. He gave tours sometimes, but his boss let him work in the gift shop or at the ticket counter most of the time, where there's less talking.

Ranger Eddie came to see me when he got home. He offered to take me to school and help me move into my dorm, since my school starts a week before his and we can spend some time catching up.

Aug 27

I am so glad Eddie came to get me! It was easy throwing everything into the back of his dad's pickup truck, strapping it all down, kissing everyone goodbye, and taking off.

I had so much to tell him! I told him about my disastrous career as a freshman. My plans to be a philosophy major. My summer at McDonald's. My Jane Austen style relationships with Darcy and Professor Jacobson.

"You and your Jane Austen," he shook his head at me.

"What's wrong with Jane Austen?" I demanded to know.

"Those are stories, Beth." Of course a guy who had known me since 6th grade couldn't adapt to my new name. "This is real life. Life isn't a romance novel."

"It can be," I insisted. "In fact, my life was very much like a romance in both cases. Very much like *Pride and Prejudice* and *Sense and Sensibility*, even. It's just that it didn't come out that way in the end."

"So you're saying the stories were right, but the endings came out wrong?"

I thought about it. "Yeah, I guess something like that."

"I think your precious Jane Austen is giving you unrealistic expectations." He gave me an earnest look. "Now you've got me worrying about you, Beth."

I couldn't decide whether I should be insulted or flattered by his concern. "You think I don't know how to distinguish fact from fiction?"

"That's kind of overstating the matter, and you know it," he said calmly. "But, it's a good question. You can tell fact from fiction, right?"

"Of course I can. But if you look at this more philosophically, all characters are an extension of the author. So instead of talking about facts, let's talk about truths. Jane Austen's characters were never real, but there's a truth to what she writes about."

"You say that, but didn't her life end rather differently than her novels?" he glanced at me skeptically.

"I..." He was right. Jane didn't get married and live happily ever after like the characters in her stories did. She must have come to her literary conclusions because of something she observed somewhere along the line, right? "You just don't understand."

"No, I probably don't." He flashed this smile at me that made it hard for me to be angry with him. "Maybe it's a guy thing. Or maybe it's a Janeite thing."

"So, tell me how your freshman year went?" I decided the best thing to do was change the subject completely. "It's sad that our schools are less than an hour apart, and we never saw each other once last year."

"I saw you on Facebook," he pointed out.

"Not the same."

"You're right." He spent the rest of the drive telling me about his year of English 101 and Science 101 and Math 101 and History 101. Before he left, we made promises to each other that this year we'll make time to see each other. After I hugged him goodbye, I lurked in the doorway and watched him walk down the hall. Suddenly it struck me hard that, wow, he's really cute! Park rangering was good for him. He's all lean and tan and muscular. His arms and shoulders in particular look really good. He's actually hot!

Aug 28

My new roommate turned up an hour or two after Eddie left. She's this tall, amazingly buxom girl named Justine. She seems really fun. But, the first thing she did was let me know she's not going to be around much.

"I hope you don't mind a private room," she said, dropping her box of stuff on the empty bed and coming over to shake my hand. "I'm really not going to be here. I'm Justine, my boyfriend John will be here in a minute."

"Nice to meet you, I'm Lizzie," I introduced myself. "Why aren't you going to be here?"

"John has a place off campus, I'm really going to be living with him," she explained. "Our parents would have a fit if we got an apartment together, so as far as they know, this is my official residence."

"Ah, I see." This could be a good thing, having a room to myself! Although Anne had always been good company. It was a shame she moved into her sorority now; I wouldn't have minded rooming with her again.

"So if my parents ever come around looking for me, tell them you saw me an hour ago," she told me.

"Sure," I reassured her. "I've got your back."

"Here's John," she introduced the stocky man with the cheerful face who walked in with a couple more boxes.

"Hey," he grunted to me while he put the boxes down.

"Hey," I answered back, then offered, "Can I help you unpack or something?"

"Sure, hang these up, and be kind of messy about it," she handed me her towels. "My parents won't believe it if anything is too tidy."

"Well, you can always complain that I keep straightening up after you, and then you can't find anything," I offered. I hung up the towels, and then tried to make them look a little askew. It actually isn't easy trying to make it look convincingly messy.

"I'm just going to make the bed, and keep a few things here that I don't need. Everything else we're taking to John's place," she told me.

"Okay," I said. "Well, if there's nothing else I can help you with, I'm gonna go look around a little. Nice meeting you," I said.

She smiled and waved. "Yeah, nice meeting you, too. Thanks for having my back."

"What are roomies for," I answered, then headed out of the room and down the hall.

The sophomore dorms are nicer and newer than the freshman dorms. I guess it hasn't been that many years since the school started requiring that all sophomores have to live on campus. I assume it's some sort of money thing. Or I suppose it could be a safety thing.

Once again, there are lounges on each floor, and a bigger common room on the first floor. This place has a more deliberately contemporary feeling to it. Everything in my other dorm had sort of a lack of style, everything was utilitarian. I imagine it was like the Soviet Union in the 1960s. Here, the front of the building has a giant glass wall up the center, where the lounges on each floor are. The chairs and desks are plain, but with an element of style to them. The handles on the furniture have a curve to them that goes beyond mere utility.

While I wandered around, there were people everywhere, carrying boxes, tubs, crates, bags, pushing giant laundry tubs, anything you could possibly transport stuff in. There was even a girl who had her things tied up inside a sheet. Kind of clever, if you think about it.

I recognize a few people from last year, but I don't know most people. Which makes sense. If you're going to house every freshman and sophomore on your campus, that's a lot of people to throw together.

I decided to get my purse and find some dinner, and got back in the elevator to go up to my room, when someone yelled "Hold the door!" I stopped the door with my arm, and in walked Lon.

"Hey, I know you," I said by way of greeting.

"Yes, I guess you do," he said.

There was this awkward silence as the doors closed. "Ten, please," he said.

I pushed the button. "You're on the same floor as me, again."

"Well, then, I guess I'll bump into you again sometime."

"I'm sure you could calculate the probability of that with ease," I said. I realized that I had just called him a nerd to his face. Or, maybe he just took it that I called him smart. Who knows. But it made me feel like I ought to say something else. "Thanks again for your help last year. I passed calculus."

"Congratulations."

We both kind of stared at the numbers on the elevator display. This thing was really slow. Of course it didn't help when people got on at floor two, then got off at five. Someone else needed to stop at seven. Finally, we made it to our floor.

As we stepped off the elevator, I had a realization. "Hey, so what are you doing here? Aren't you in a fraternity? Why aren't you rooming with your frat house?"

"Too expensive." He shifted the box in his arms. "This is heavy. I'll see you later sometime."

"Yeah, see you later." Once again, his room was on one side of the elevators, mine was on the other side. For a crazy moment, I almost asked him if he wanted to go get dinner with me. Then I thought better of it. If Justine and John were still around, I ought to eat with them, before they disappeared and I never saw them again.

Aug 29

Eddie is being as good as his word about not vanishing from my life again. He texted me today.

Hey

                                        Hey, yourself

What're you doing?

                            Buying my books. What're you
                            doing?

Throwing my stuff in the
truck. Talk about déjà vu.

                            Thanks again for taking me to school.

No charge.

                            Good, cuz I can't afford too much.

Are you going to work at
the law library again?

                            I hope so. If they'll take me back. I
                            love that job. Especially if I can get
                            evening hours again. I get paid to sit
                            and do my homework.

Sweet. So what classes do
philosophy majors take?

                            Well, I don't know about other
                            philosophy majors, but I'm taking

Morality and its Critics, Introduction to Eastern Philosophy, Introduction to Ethics, Art History, and Spanish.

You already sound like a philosopher. So is there an "Ethics to Art History" class you take next semester?

Maybe. Art history has nothing to do with philosophy. I just wanted to take it.

Well, good luck with all of them. I need to throw my last things in the truck, say goodbye to my folks, and drive. TTYL

K, bye.

After I got my books back to my room, I went over to the law library to see if I still had a job there. My boss looked me over. "Are you dating any law students?" she asked me.

"No," I told her. I thought about reminding her that the problem was that I hadn't been dating Darcy Fitzwilliam. Then I figured that the less I said, the better.

"That's a pity, if you were dating one, then the others wouldn't be asking you out and getting irritated with you while you're working." I could see now that she was amused by me. I guessed that meant I was hired back.

"You could put me on a shift when there are fewer single guys in here?" I suggested to her.

"Wouldn't it be better if I put you on a shift with the maximum number of single guys?" she eyed me speculatively. "So that one of them would become your boyfriend and protect you from the rest?"

"You're assuming I'm interested in guys," I pointed out to her. "What if I'm into girls?"

"There is no way I can possibly ask that question, and still call myself a professional," she pointed out, arching her brow.

"I swear to you, no one of either gender is going to make a scene with me the way Darcy Fitzwilliam did last year," I promised. "This is a whole new year, and I'm not going to have anyone pestering me." I thought of Eddie. "Besides, I might be sort of starting a thing with an old friend of mine. If it works out and I'm seeing someone, no one can take offense at my saying no to a date, because I'm already taken."

"I see. Well, good luck with that. Give me a copy of your schedule and I'll put you on the rotation starting next week."

I did a little dance as I went down the stairs and left the building. It feels like some sort of small victory over Mr. Fitzwilliam that I still have a job, despite his trying to get me in trouble.

Sept 1

It turns out there's another benefit to having Justine as my roommate. Not only is she not around much, so I practically have my own place, she also has a car, and she's invited me to use it!"

"Okay, so, I realize that all I ever do when I see you is ask you for favors," she said to me today, which is the first time I've seen her since we moved in.

"You are kind of demanding that way," I agreed with her cheerfully. "What is it you need me to do, now?"

"Sort of keep a little bit of an eye on my car for me?" she pointed out the window.

I walked over to stand with her. It was hard to tell where she was pointing. There's a big parking lot behind our dorm, but there's a row of trees between us and it.

"Can you see the old white car, over on the left in the first row? It's a Chevy."

I thought that was kind of a vague description. "A Chevy what?"

"Oh, I don't know. It's old, whatever it is. I don't think they make them anymore." She handed me a set of car keys. "My dad just got it for me, because he thinks I'll come home more often if I have a car. I told him that's not gonna happen, because I've got school, and a job, and I'm busy, and what am I gonna do with a car on campus? I can't park it at John's apartment, or I'll get towed. So I'm just going to leave it here. Dad gave me the money to get a pass to park in that lot all semester, but I guess someone ought to look in on it once in a while. Or drive it sometimes. If you'll take a look at it once a week or something, and make sure it hasn't been stolen or vandalized or whatever else bad can happen to a car, I'll leave the keys here, and you can drive it once in a while if you like. At the very least, put it in a different parking spot from time to time so people don't think it's abandoned."

I couldn't believe my luck. Free use of a car? "Sure, I can help you out. But before you leave, you'd better give me your cell number. If I ever need to reach you because your parents are here, or there's something wrong with the car, I don't have your number right now."

Justine whipped out her phone, and gave me her number, and John's number, and John's housemate's number, and her work number, and a couple of other phone numbers that I didn't even understand quite what they were for. But they were all ways to reach her, if need be.

Sept 9

Okay, so hanging out with Eddie is fun, but this is going to be frustrating. Now that I've figured out that he's really hot, I thought I'd try to get him to notice me. Anne's best pair of high-heeled boots with the lacing up the back is apparently no match for the charms of this girl from his English lit class. Last night he came into town to grab dinner with me, but then all he wanted to talk about was Katie this, and Katie that, and Katie is so smart, and Katie is a music major, and Katie is going to play clarinet with an orchestra someday and Katie was writing a song on the piano for her music composition class.

"Can we talk about something besides Katie?" I finally asked him.

"Oh, sorry. Sure. How's your week been?"

"Good. I talked to my parents last night, they say hello."

"That's great. I got to meet Katie's parents. She'd forgotten her guitar, so they brought it to her. She says playing the guitar relaxes her when she's having trouble thinking."

So much for not talking about Katie!

I'm going to need a better plan of attack. Unfortunately, I have no idea what that might be. I'm certainly not about to turn into a music major. I sucked at the violin when I played it in the school orchestra, and I'm not going to be composing sonatas in his honor.

I think for now I'm going to simply stay the course. Katie may be talented with music, but Tiffany helped me buy a push-up bra that's got padding at least an inch thick which gives me amazing cleavage and loaned me a purple leopard print top that, when worn with said bra, she swears will stop traffic. Katie may have a collection of musical instruments, and she's a virtuoso on all of them, but Anne's got a collection of high-heeled shoes that she says I can borrow all I like. I'm determined to rock those things out.

Sept 30

I got to meet Katie today. Dammit, she's not only talented, she's also very pretty, and was extremely nice to me! I really didn't want to like her.

Eddie invited me to go to a concert with him. I didn't realize until after we were seated that it was her concert. I mean, how was I supposed to know that music majors will perform a concert when they've only been back in school for a month? I was so excited when he asked me. Anne came over and took two hours helping me get ready. I was completely dolled out. Hair, makeup, dress with keyholes in the front and back, shoes that say "I demand that you check out my legs. Nice, huh?" I was perfect. I even had a necklace that had a little pendant that sat exactly in the middle of the keyhole, saying "Yeah, you want to stare at my cleavage. You know you do."

I found Justine's car, and made up songs praising her name as I took it on a joyride. Eddie and I had dinner at this cute little Vietnamese place just off campus. The service is slow, but the food is really good. And cheap. One of my teachers last year used to love to say, "Good, fast, cheap. Pick two…" There are so many times that the expression comes to mind!

Then we walked over to the concert hall, and I realized it was on campus. "So, what are we going to see?" I'd never actually asked him. I'd just said yes when he invited me out.

"It's the fall concert for the school's wind ensemble, I think. They're going to be playing Gershwin's 'Rhapsody in Blue,' 'American in Paris,' and a few other things, and I know how much you love Gershwin."

I was thrilled that he remembered. I did a paper on Gershwin for English class in high school. "I do love 'Rhapsody in Blue'!" I smiled up at him. "It was very thoughtful of you to invite me."

"Katie says she's the soloist for it. This is going to be fantastic!" he grinned down at me. I tried not to let my smile show that I was unhappy with that bit of news.

"That's awesome!" I said to cover my disappointment.

The lights dimmed, and the orchestra came in and the musicians took their places. "There she is," Eddie whispered to me.

Damn. Damn, damn, damn. She looked tall, and she had on the typical white blouse and black skirt. A short black skirt, and heels that were probably half an inch taller than the ones I had on. And those shoes said "Hey, audience! I dare you to concentrate on the music while I'm showing off these shapely legs."

The concert was good. Of course it was. They played selections from *Porgy and Bess*, and "American in Paris." Then, after an intermission where I got to hear all about what a great musician Katie is, we went back in. The lights went down. The orchestra came back in, giving Katie another chance to show off her terrific legs, and then she put the clarinet to her lips.

Shit. Shit, shit, shit. The first notes of "Rhapsody" came trembling out from her clarinet. It's the sexiest music ever written, soulful and erotic and passionate. And she played it with soul, eroticism, and passion. My heart was beating madly while she played. I was breathing heavily. I think I was even blushing. Eddie was holding my hand, and squeezing it just a little too hard. I wished it was because he knew how much I loved this piece, but I knew better. He had the hots for the musician playing it. She could have been playing "Baa, Baa, Black Sheep," and he would have been squeezing my hand equally hard.

By the end, I had to admit, I couldn't hate her anymore. It had been a brilliant rendition of "Rhapsody." I kept finding myself holding my breath. I was in tears when the lights came up. "Wasn't she amazing?" Eddie gushed. All I could do was nod.

We waited in the lobby after the concert. "Eddie!" Katie called to him. And, wouldn't you know it, on top of everything else, she has a foreign accent. "I'm so glad you made the concert! And this must be Lizzie." She turned a dazzling smile on me. "Eddie has told me so much about you. You are every bit as beautiful as he said you are." She kissed both my cheeks.

My head was in a jumble. I wanted to hate her, but she was holding onto my hand and smiling at me with these perfect teeth and bright, friendly eyes. And not only did she call me beautiful, she just told me that Eddie told her I was beautiful.

"Thanks," I tried to smile back at her as nicely as she was smiling at me. "And you are every bit as talented as Eddie says you are."

"Eddie is very kind to me, I'm sure." She smiled up at Eddie, and my heart plummeted to my stomach. If she's gone on him, and he's gone on her, I might as well give up. They'll be dating by this time next week.

Oct 14

Well, it's been two weeks, and Eddie has no news to report. Interestingly, he's asked me to go with him to a party at Katie's house. You would think he would be trying to get Katie alone, not bringing another girl along.

"Why do you want me to come with you to Katie's party?" I asked. I didn't see any reason not to be blunt about this.

"Katie asked me to invite you," he told me. "She likes you, and since you're my best friend, she says she wants to get to know you better."

Great. My heart sank. She's checking him out, and checking me out as a part of the family. Then I started to wonder. If you're interested in a guy, do you go inviting the competition? Maybe this was her way of putting me in the middle, because she's not interested in him.

I guessed there was only one way to find out. "Okay, I'll go with you to this party."

"Oh, good," Eddie sounded relieved. "It's going to be mostly people from the orchestra, and I won't know many of them. It will be so nice to have someone with me that I know."

Oct 15

So, I borrowed Justine's car again tonight, drove up to Eddie's place, picked him up, and we went to Katie's party. Like he said, it was mostly people from the orchestra. I would have thought that a bunch of musicians who want to be in concert orchestras when they grow up would all be kind of stuffy, but it turns out that wasn't the case at all. They were actually a really rowdy bunch. Raunchy, too. There was a game of strip poker going on in one room. And lots of booze. I've participated in my share of illegal drinking, but even I was amazed at the variety of alcohol they had at the bar set up in the basement. The Greeks got nothing on these musicians!

Katie and two guys came and found Eddie and me while we were sort of wandering around the house, taking everything in. "Why don't you come with us," they invited us mysteriously.

"Sure," Eddie said. Whenever Katie was around, he didn't have eyes for anyone else. We followed them into the back yard, where there was a bonfire burning. There were people sitting on the grass putting something in their mouth, and a tall guy with three days' growth was handing out little tin foil packets.

"There she is!" several people exclaimed at once when Katie approached the bonfire.

"Here I is," she answered, and took three little tin foil packets from the scruffy man. She handed one to me, one to Eddie, and unfolded her own foil packet to reveal a little white piece of paper.

"What is it?" Eddie asked.

"You've never dropped acid?" she asked him with an incredulous laugh.

Now, maybe this sounds hypocritical coming from someone who has had plenty of Long Islands when I'm not 21 yet, but this made me totally uncomfortable. At least alcohol is legal in some contexts, but LSD isn't legal for anyone. "Come on, Eddie, it's chilly out here. Let's go back inside," I tugged on his arm.

Eddie didn't budge. Katie opened his foil for him and held up the paper. "Put this under your tongue and leave it there," she told him, talking slightly funny from her own paper. "Keep it there for about an hour to be safe. Don't swallow it, or it won't work."

Eddie just looked at her for a second. I could feel the tension in his body. He didn't want to be there, but he also didn't want to leave. He looked at Katie for what seemed like a long time, then he took the paper from her and followed her instructions.

When he opened his mouth, I let go of his arm and went back in the house. I'd rather be playing strip poker with complete strangers than taking illegal substances. I headed for the basement to get a drink, then realized that I was the one who drove to the party. Well, if I had one drink, I wouldn't be too intoxicated to drive. We weren't going to be leaving right away. While I was enjoying a very strong rum and coke I discovered there was also plenty of food, so I wouldn't have to drink on an empty stomach.

Before I got in even a single bite of pizza, however, the party ended in a most interesting manner. Katie's parents came home a day early. I guess they caught an earlier flight, or something. Anyway, they walked in, and it turned out to be quite the surprise to everyone. There was a whole lot of shouting from the parents while we all scrambled to our cars. I'm sure Katie is in plenty of trouble.

I could hardly speak to Eddie while I hustled him out the door. He was totally high, and exhibiting every symptom they described in health class in high school. He was so mellow and relaxed it was hard for me to guide him to the car. He kept wandering off to examine odd things, and make even odder comments. "Look at all the art on the lawn, they should make clothes like that." His speech was all slurred. While I fumbled for my car keys, he announced he'd discovered new constellations.

"Look, over there, it looks like a clipper ship. That's fitting, isn't it, since sailors used to navigate by the stars?" He put his arm around me, and pointed somewhere else in the sky. "And over there, that looks like one of the shuttles we used to send up." He gave my shoulders a squeeze. "Remember how much we used to love going to the planetarium?"

Now, normally, I would have been thrilled to have his arm around me, and talking sentimentally of things we did in high school together. But escaping the wrath of Katie's parents did not seem like a good time to get romantic. "I love the planetarium. If you get in the car, we can drive someplace where we can see the stars better."

"That works." He got in the car. I closed the car door for him, and walked around to the driver's side. His hands were shaking so much, I had to buckle his seat belt for him. He giggled while I did it.

"What's so funny?" I asked.

"I have this horrible urge to say 'groovy' a lot. Like they did in the 60s."

I was starving, and afraid I was still too drunk to be driving, so I stopped at this little burger place that was open 24 hours.

He seemed to be more interested in the words on the menu than their meanings, so I just ordered for him as well as for me. Then I couldn't get him to eat anything.

"Aren't you supposed to get the munchies, like Shaggy and Scooby-Doo?" I joked, but I was actually miffed. And scared. Could people get arrested for obviously having LSD in their bloodstream? I didn't know. Would I get arrested for being with him while he was high? I didn't know that, either.

"Jinkies," Eddie giggled.

The plan had been for me to crash on his couch that night, but I was upset enough I knew I'd be fine for the drive home. I got him into his apartment, said good night, and left. I spent the entire drive home thinking that I didn't like Katie's influence on Eddie. He's usually such a serious guy, and I'm sure there are plenty of people who'd say maybe it was good for someone to loosen him up a little, but I still don't like it.

Nov 12

I didn't ever want to see Katie again, and I wasn't too sure about wanting to see Eddie again, either. But I didn't get a choice in the matter.

After a month of communications silence, they came to see me tonight. They didn't even tell me they were coming. They showed up as I was getting off work at the library. I might have told them both to kiss off, except for the fact that I saw Darcy Fitzwilliam this afternoon, which put me in a really bad place. We didn't say anything, we just sort of glared at each other. Having two people gush over me and say how glad they are to see me was like a balm. I have to admit that while I wasn't sure I wanted to see either of them, I was glad to have the company, and the distraction.

"So where do you guys want to go to dinner?" I asked. "And what are you up to tonight?"

"We're kidnapping you for a night of fun and frolic." Katie held up three tickets. "That is, if you want to go with us to see the Metallica concert."

I was about to say no, because I had a lot of homework. But the homework will have to get done tomorrow. I mean, a Metallica concert?

We grabbed dinner at the little Thai place across the street from the arena, and had fun sitting in the window, watching the traffic get heavier, and heavier, and heavier.

"That's why you asked me to join you. You wanted to be able to use the parking lot by my dorm," I commented.

"Well, yeah," Eddie laughed at me. "It's not because we wanted to hang out with you."

"I will confess, you weren't the first people that came to mind when these tickets fell into my possession," Katie admitted with a disgustingly disarming smile as we joined the throngs of people walking to the arena. "My stand partner is the one who gave them to me. She was supposed to be going with her sisters, but their aunt passed away, so they're on their way to Chicago for a funeral. I asked a couple other people from the wind ensemble, but people either already had tickets, or other commitments."

"So you're saying we're losers because we don't already have plans for tonight," I hoped I sounded like I was kidding, although I actually was kind of miffed.

"You know that's not what she meant," Eddie defended her. I should have known better; of course Eddie knows how to read my voice. He knows me too well, and for too long. I can't say things without him knowing what I'm thinking.

"Sure it is," Katie laughed. I could tell she was teasing, but Eddie gave her a very hurt look, which she didn't seem to see. "But I'm glad you're both losers since it would be a shame if these tickets went to waste."

"I'm very glad to oblige, since there's no way I could afford to go otherwise." Eddie answered sincerely. "Being a poor college student and all."

"Well, it's temporary. We're only poor students for four years, and then we get to go make our way in the world. I intend to be able to afford all the concert tickets I want in a year."

"That will be hard to do on a concert musician's salary, I should think," I commented.

"Well, another income will help. I intend to marry well," Katie said it very matter-of-factly. I could see she really meant it. She means to find a rich man. How very 19th century of her. I could hear the echoes of Mrs. Bennett talking about how much money Mr. Bingley was worth.

"Then I suppose you won't be interested in marrying me. I'm just going to be a poor clergyman," Eddie announced.

Both of us stared at him. I hadn't known he was planning to go into the seminary. How on earth would I guess that? He hadn't told me, and doing illegal drugs last time I saw him didn't seem like clergyman behavior.

Katie was my partner in disbelief. "Poor clergyman? Considering the wealth and power commanded by churches, I should hardly think that ministers are generally poor. Unless you're planning on being some sort of monk," she answered archly.

"Ministers are comfortable, but not rich. I'm never going to have my own private jet," Eddie said. "And with concert tickets running over a hundred dollars apiece, I don't know how many concert tickets I'll be able to afford in the course of a year. It might be a lot. It might not be. I'm imagining that by the time I pay for my wife's car payment, and the kid's clothes, and shoes, and school tuition, there won't be time or money left for any concerts."

"If you have fewer kids, there's more money for concerts," Katie pointed out. We were clambering through the stadium rows to our seats; it struck me as a funny place to be having this conversation. "Or, if you go into a career that makes more money, if indeed the church pays so poorly, you can afford kids and concert tickets. Why don't you become a lawyer instead of a preacher? You still get to make speeches in front of an audience. And there's so many directions you can go from there if you want to be using your powers of speech to make the world a better place. You can handle divorces, or defend innocent men who have been accused of crimes, or become a judge. Or you can run for office. I think most senators and presidents have been lawyers."

Eddie pretty much ignored me as we sat down. "I have no interest in going into politics or law. I'd rather offer spiritual guidance to people than break up marriages and create more children from broken homes."

Katie looked at him with a certain amount of contempt. "So you think it's better for children to live with two parents who do nothing but fight all the time?"

Eddie was not cowed. "The idea is that a minister helps counsel people so they don't fight."

Katie shook her head. "Good luck with that. My parents are both very religious, and they fight all the time. They used to shout at each other in the car on the way to church, and on the way home from church. I used to pray that they'd get a divorce, so I wouldn't have to listen to them fighting anymore. But it never worked out. That's why I stopped praying altogether. It doesn't work."

Eddie looked at her with compassion. "God obviously had other plans."

"Well, I can't say I'm impressed with 'plans' that involve two people being miserable, but staying together for the sake of God – and the children," she answered.

"That's why you have to have faith," he insisted.

The debate would probably have gone on all night, except that the lights went down, and the crowd began screaming in anticipation.

All through the concert, I had one nagging thought in the back of my mind; I had just left *Pride and Prejudice* and *Sense and Sensibility* behind me, but now I seemed to being living in *Mansfield Park*. I suppose I should find that comforting. After all, eventually Edmund stops mooning over Miss Crawford and realizes Fanny's value. Maybe it will work out the same for me.

Nov 16

What a birthday I'm having! I had lunch with my ex-roommate Anne, whom I haven't seen in a while, and she got me this cute little hat. It turns out, it matches my coat perfectly. Allie and her mom met me after class to give me a really big coffee mug with Jane Austen quotes all over it. Katie mailed me the Blu-ray of *Persuasion* – the version with Amanda Root and Ciaran Hinds. I love that version! It's totally smoking hot. Tiffany always describes that kiss at the end as "the kiss you can feel in your thighs."

Eddie drove in to take me to dinner for my birthday even though it's Wednesday and he's got class in the morning at 8:00. Now that's love, wouldn't you say?

I waited in front of my dorm so he wouldn't have to bother parking the car. I jumped in, and off we went.

"Okay, so I'm driving, but where am I going?" he asked.

"Let's get off campus. I've eaten at every single place within walking distance, there's nothing new to try around here."

"That sounds good. But it doesn't answer the question of where I'm going, and when I need to turn the steering wheel instead of going straight," he smiled at me.

"Oh. Yeah. Take a right here," I directed. "Let's go out to the mall. I haven't been to a BW3 in forever."

"Sure." He glanced over at me while we were stopped at the light. "That's a really cute hat. It suits your face beautifully."

"Thanks! My old roommate gave it to me for my birthday." I flipped down the visor to check it out in the little mirror.

"It's cute. Katie has one almost exactly like it."

Damn. She's not even along, and she's still in the car with us.

After we were settled in our seats at BW3, Eddie pulled a rectangular package out of the pocket of his jacket.

"Here, you might as well have your birthday present while we're waiting," he slid it across the table to me.

It was a DVD shaped package. I was really making out in the DVD department! "Sweet!" I unwrapped it, appreciating the purple and silver wrapping paper before I tore into it. It was another copy of *Persuasion*. The same version Katie had sent me. I started laughing as soon as I saw it.

"What is it?" he asked.

I suddenly regretted having laughed. I didn't want to tell him about the duplicate copies, and the source.

"I love this movie," I answered, hoping that would be enough.

It wasn't. "But why were you laughing?" he persisted.

"Well," I couldn't think of anything else to say, so I guessed I'd have to tell him the truth. "I got a package from Katie yesterday. She sent me the same movie for my birthday."

Predictably, he was all smiles when I said Katie's name. "She did? Wow, great minds think alike. That was very thoughtful of her. She really likes you. I'm so glad of it." He reached across the table, and pulled my DVD back. "Tell you what, you keep hers, and I'll exchange this for you. What would you like? Are you missing any other Jane Austen movies? I know you had them all on VHS. What haven't you replaced yet?"

"I don't have the Keira Knightly version of *Pride and Prejudice*, but I'm not sure I want it. Donald Sutherland's portrayal of Mr. Bennett is a disgrace. If you want a challenge, there's a version of *Emma* that's only available in the UK, with Kate Beckinsale playing Emma. I really want that." I tried to keep up my end of the conversation with enthusiasm, but I had some trouble faking it. I was so disheartened by his excitement at finding out that he and Katie bought me the same thing. This sucks.

Nov 18

Today I can't decide if things suck less, or more now. I stayed up pretty much all night, texting with Eddie. He and Katie had a discussion about religion that upset him. He wants to be a minister, she told him she's Catholic.

I said, "What's the problem, you both believe in God, right?"

He said "It's a big problem, you can't be a Methodist minister with a Catholic wife. How can you preach to a congregation if your own wife doesn't subscribe to the same faith?"

Great. So he's thinking about marrying Katie. I asked him if it wasn't a little early to talk about marriage, since they weren't even officially boyfriend and girlfriend yet. He said that if he knew what he wanted, he didn't see the point in beating around the bush. None of this made me any happier, of course. But I kept on being the good best friend, asking him questions and making him talk about it. Every answer was ripping me up inside, but I kept on going, since he needed to talk. At least I get beaucoup "Best Friend" points, right? About 3 in the morning, I think, he told me how great I am, and that I'm the only person in the world he can really talk to. Still channeling *Mansfield Park*, I told him "You can always tell me anything." He did say "I know," before he went back to talking about Katie and how much she's hurt him. So I'm sleepwalking through my classes today, and all I can think of while I'm supposed to be taking notes in lecture is that boys are stupid.

Nov 18 (again)

Okay, so now I've had a long messaging chat on Facebook with Katie. It doesn't make me feel any better. She is obviously just as pleased as Eddie that the two of them were thinking alike, and bought me the same birthday present. Dear me, how intimate. Her word for it. Sigh. She went on about what a sweet and thoughtful guy he is. What was I supposed to say? He's actually a big dumb jerk when you get to know him better?

Hmm. Maybe that is what I should have said. Damn.

Nov 19

I wish Wendy and I had a relationship like Jane did with Cassandra. Which is pretty much the same relationship as Lizzie and Jane in *Pride and Prejudice*. Even Marianne and Elinor have a mostly supportive relationship. When the girls have problems, they confide in each other. When their fortunes seem to be up, they are happy for each other.

My sister? Ha.

She called me today, to wish me a belated happy birthday. I thanked her, she told me about all the gossip of what was going on with the senior class, and my favorite teachers, and my least favorite teachers. She told me she was thinking about breaking up with John, her current boyfriend, because he was being a jerk. Meanwhile, the president of the chess club asked her out, and she wanted to say yes.

"Well, you'll have to break up with John before you go out with this other guy," I told her.

"Why? I'm not married to him," she protested. "Can't I just go for coffee with Patrick, to see if he's worth breaking up with John?"

"How would you feel if he did the same thing to you?" I asked.

There was silence for a while on the other end of the phone. "I think he already has. That's why I'm wondering about breaking up with him."

"Ah, I see." I wasn't sure what advice I could give at that point.

"You were smart not to date anybody in high school," she told me grumpily.

"I'm trying to make up for that now," I told her.

"Well, between the rich jerky guy, and the professor who wasn't interested in you, I don't think you're making much progress," she said.

"Gee, thanks," I said dryly. This is the support I get for listening to her romantic woes? I decided to let it go, and get on with what I was trying to tell her. "I wasn't thinking about them, I'm kind of seeing a lot of Eddie Jameson these days."

"You're dating Eddie? I assume his acne has cleared up?" Leave it to a little sister to remember those things.

"Yeah, it's a lot better. Didn't you see him when he picked me up to take me back to school?"

"I had a soccer game! I can't believe you forgot that I said goodbye to you first thing that morning."

"Oh, yeah. That's right." Still, I refused to let her irritate me. I'm supposed to be the more mature sister, after all. "Sorry, I was thinking about Eddie, not you. His summer as a park ranger did wonders for him. You wouldn't believe how hot he is."

"Well, next time you go out, text me a picture of the two of you," she suggested.

It was my turn for a long pause. "Well, we're not going out, as in, going out, going out…"

"Well, if you're not dating him, what did you mean about seeing him?" she asked impatiently.

"It's complicated," I explained, realizing it was no explanation at all.

"So you're not really going out, you just hang out once in a while. Like you were supposed to go to prom together because neither of you had a date, except you had the flu and didn't get to go at all."

"That last part has nothing to do with the rest of the story," I protested.

"Well, that's what happened," I swear I could hear her shrugging over the phone.

"We would have gone to prom, yes. And, yes, I guess it is kind of the same thing. I'm just hoping it won't be. If I can manage to edge out the competition."

"You've got competition? You're gonna get creamed."

"Gee, thanks for the vote of confidence. Yes, he's interested in this girl named Katie. She's kind of a bitch, she's totally wrong for him, I'm just waiting until he figures it out."

"He might not figure it out, you know. He wasn't that smart. Didn't he get, like, straight C's your last semester in high school?"

"That was high school. And there's a big difference between book smart and being smart about people," I argued.

"Maybe," she sounded dubious.

"Look, remember *Mansfield Park*? Edmund seems to be so in love with Mary Crawford, who is totally wrong for him. Eventually he figures it out, and he realizes that Fanny Price has always been there for him."

"Well, what if Eddie in real life isn't as people smart as Edmund in fictional life? This is real life, not fiction. People don't change in real life. They don't have epiphanies and suddenly become better people. And they certainly don't become smarter."

"Sure, they do," I insisted. "People can grow. And when they make mistakes, they become wiser. That's different than smarter."

"You think that, if you want to." She was always more cynical than me, I suppose. I shouldn't have been surprised by her sarcastic response. "But when you come crying to me that Eddie has disobeyed the Jane Austen plot and married this chick who is totally wrong for him, I'm going to remind you about this conversation."

"I'm sure you will," I was pretty miffed. "Talk to you later. Thanks for the belated birthday call." The problem with cell phones, you can't slam the phone down to hang up. I remember this phone we used to have when we were really little. Mom would slam the receiver back onto the cradle, and it would make this loud ringing bang that said 'I am so mad at you!'

Nov 23

Well! Here's a turn of events. Eddie is going away on a retreat at a seminary over Thanksgiving weekend. He met up with some other guys here in town, so he came over to have lunch with me before he headed out for the weekend.

"So, what are you going to do on this holy retreat of yours?" I asked.

"Examine our consciences, ourselves, our relationship with God," he said.

"So you're going to drink, smoke pot, and talk about women?" I joked. He looked at me.

"Well, yeah, there might be some of that," he admitted after a brief pause. "Just because we're there to talk about whether we really and truly want to dedicate our lives to God doesn't mean we're not going to talk about other aspects of our lives."

"Well, if you ever get the chance while you're busy talking about Katie, you can talk about me, too, a little bit. Maybe one of those other seminary guys would be interested in dating me," I joked.

"I can talk about you if you want me to. After all, you're my best friend, my surrogate sister, and there's this place in my heart that belongs only to you."

I couldn't speak for happiness for a moment. That was his fancy way of saying he loved me. Ok, only as his best friend, but didn't couples at the altar always say that "today I'm marrying my best friend?"

"Thanks," I finally said. "In case you were wondering, the feeling's mutual."

That was lunchtime. By dinnertime, who should pop up and say she wanted to go shopping with me, but Katie! This is ridiculous. I didn't have a good excuse not to go with her, so the next thing you know I'm in her car, we're off to the mall, and we're wandering around trying on boots and buying the same shade of nail polish.

"So, did you get to see Ed on his way out of town?" she asked me while we were admiring the display in the window of Victoria's Secret.

I was instantly on the alert. "Yeah, he came and had lunch with me before he headed out on this retreat," I told her.

"He said he was going to. Did you have a good time?"

"Yeah, it was nice," I answered. I realized that she was pimping me for information, so I decided to say as little as possible, to see how much she wanted to talk about him.

"Did he tell you much about this retreat he's going on?" she asked.

"A little. Not much in the way of details." I answered.

"He didn't tell me too much about it, either," she volunteered.

"Maybe it's mystery Methodist rituals, and they're forbidden to talk about it. Like being in the Masons," I said.

"Maybe. I'm worried about him. I don't think this is a good career path for him to take. He's smart, he's a hard worker, he can do so much better for himself than being a little country parson at a Methodist church."

"There are churches in cities, too," I pointed out.

"Yes, but somehow that seems even worse," she frowned. "Living expenses are higher, and there must be more problems in the city than in the country."

"People have problems." I refused to give her any satisfaction. "I don't think it matters where you live, people always have problems."

"That's why I think he should go into law, instead of the church," she grabbed my arm enthusiastically, "so that he can help people in a more substantial way."

"And get paid better?" I asked.

"Well, yes, that goes without saying," she agreed with me.

Somehow I hadn't expected her to be quite so honest in her greed. This was obviously all about money, and her ability to get what she wants out of Eddie. And she said before, she wants money. "I don't think Eddie cares about money."

"But he does care about helping people. You've known him so much longer than I have, why don't you talk to him? I'm sure you can talk him out of this crazy idea of becoming a minister. You work at the law school, don't you? Don't you have any literature you can give him with information about a career in law?"

I really didn't want to talk to her about Eddie anymore. "I don't think so, but I'll look next time I'm at work," I lied. "So where should we go to dinner? There's a Ruby Tuesdays right here at the end of this section of the mall. Unless you'd rather go up to the food court."

Nov 28

Well, it's over! Eddie came back from his retreat, and he asked Katie out on a date. An official date. She said yes, they went out for the classic dinner and a movie, and apparently it was a disaster. He called me up tonight as soon as he dropped her off at her dorm.

"Hi, Beth, I know it's late, but can we talk?"

"Late is when we usually do our best talking," I answered, trying not to yawn. I didn't want him to know that he woke me up.

"I'm not going to be asking Katie out on any more dates."

I was instantly awake. "Oh?"

"I took her out for dinner and a movie, and from the moment I picked her up to the moment I dropped her off, the entire evening was one big downward spiral," he sighed.

"What happened?"

"I figured out that we are absolutely incompatible."

No shit. "That's a little vague," I said aloud.

"But very accurate." I could hear him smiling at me over the phone, the way he does when he's being a smart ass.

"Well, if you've made your point and that's all you wanted to tell me, I'll go back to sleep," I said. Two can play at the smart ass game.

"I'm sorry. I didn't mean to wake you. I can hang up and talk to you later."

"Of course I'm not going to go back to sleep right now. You're upset, tell me what happened." I thought the direct approach was the way to go.

"We're such different people, and we want such different things out of life. She thinks I should be going to law school, not into the seminary."

"That's not news," I pointed out. "She's been saying that for a while. So you're telling me you haven't been listening, and you just figured it out?"

"I don't know," he almost wailed at me. "She's not the person I thought she was. She's so…cynical, and worldly, and she does illegal drugs."

"So did you, at her party," I pointed out.

"And she makes me do things that are against my better judgment, and that's not healthy. People should bring out the best in each other, not encourage the worst in each other," he observed.

I wanted to beat him about the head and shoulders about her party, and him doing drugs there, but he already got that message, loud and clear. It seemed like time to change the subject. "I'm cynical and worldly, does this mean you don't like me, either?" I asked.

"You're not that cynical. And besides, it's not the same thing."

I wanted to divert the conversation to talk about me, and why he doesn't think I'm cynical, but I wasn't sure how to do it without seeming vain. So I went with the second half of his statement. "How so? Or, should I say, how not?"

"I don't know. It's different. You make observations about people, but you're still fundamentally a kind person. She gets very critical of people for little things, and passes judgment upon them for very small infractions. She's not kind. You have the world figured out, but you don't try to force other people to conform to your world view. She seems to think that her way is the only right way."

"So you're telling me she said that you need to convert to Catholicism and become a Catholic priest, instead of a Methodist minister?"

"Well, no. But she wouldn't consider converting from Catholic to Methodist."

"You asked her, did you?"

"Well, yes."

"What did she say?"

"She told me that Methodists are fundamentally the same as Catholics, except for the thing about the priests marrying."

I was glad we were having this conversation on the phone, so he couldn't see me laughing. I had to put my phone on mute for a moment, I was afraid I was going to laugh out loud and he'd hear me.

"Are you there?"

"Sorry, yeah, dropped the phone. Cell phones aren't very good for cradling against one's shoulder."

"What happened to that earpiece you had?"

"It's on my desk. I don't feel like getting out of bed to get it."

"You're in bed?"

"Of course I'm in bed. You woke me up, remember?"

"You shouldn't talk to people while you're in bed."

"Why not? It's not like you can see me sitting here in my pjs. And it's a good thing, too. My hair is probably a mess."

"Well, maybe people can't see you, but it's still, I don't know, lascivious somehow."

"Not my fault you have a dirty mind."

"I do not have a dirty mind!"

This time I laughed out loud. "No, no you don't. Although I bet you'd been having lascivious thoughts about Katie up until this date of yours."

"She's completely wrong for me. In one evening I found out our religions are incompatible, our political affiliations are not the same, what we want out of life is not the same. She doesn't even want children. How can any woman not want children?"

"Some women don't. Children take up a lot of time and money, some women want to focus on things like careers instead. It sort of makes sense for Katie, she's very focused on her music, and she's ambitious."

"You can play clarinet and be pregnant at the same time," he answered stubbornly.

"I've never seen a concert musician on stage while nine months pregnant. It must happen, but if she doesn't want to go there, she doesn't want to go there. It makes sense for her, she's got a lot of talent and she wants to cultivate it, without distractions. Kids would be a huge distraction." I couldn't believe my ears, here I was defending Katie. On the other hand, if this was making Eddie more convinced that he was incompatible with her, that was a good thing!

"I'm done with her. I need someone I can talk to, and I'll never be able to talk to her about anything of substance."

I took a breath. Here was my opportunity. "Well, if talking is that important to you, why don't you try dating me?"

"I can't do that, that's disgusting. You're like a sister to me. It would be weird. It would feel like incest."

My heart came to a complete stop. I was sitting there in bed, leaning up against the wall, my knees to my chest, my mouth hanging open. Dating me would be disgusting to him...?

I couldn't let it go without a fight. "We're not really related, you know. It wouldn't be incest. Hell, if we were stepbrother and stepsister, we could have been raised together under one roof and it wouldn't be incest, since we're not blood related."

He sighed. "Look, Beth, I know you're trying to make me feel better, but I'm sorry, this just isn't funny."

Now I really had nothing to say. So much for the idea of being there for someone, and it blossoms into more than that. At least Edmund in *Mansfield Park* ended up realizing the value of a good listener and a loyal friend. And they were actually cousins!

"Okay, I shouldn't have called you so late, you're being weird and stupid because you're tired," Eddie said when I didn't say anything. "Thanks for listening, I'll talk to you later. Good night." He hung up.

I don't think I moved for an hour after that. I've been sitting in bed, staring out the window. I want to cry, but I can't. I feel like I've been kicked in the stomach, and I can't breathe. I want to throw up, but my body is frozen. I can't move my muscles to get to a waste paper basket, and if I could, my stomach is as frozen as the rest of me. I want a drink, but I don't exactly have a bottle of booze hidden in my dorm room. I'm going to have to remedy that.

Nov 29

When Ken saw me in Spanish class, he asked me what was wrong.

"Why do you think something's wrong?" I asked.

"Well, for starters, you plopped your books down next to me, but you haven't said anything after 'hi.' That's not like you," he said. "Then you keep sighing these big tragic sighs. Most people do not make big tragic sighs unless they're going through some tragedy."

"Sorry. I didn't realize."

"Nothing to be sorry for. But you didn't answer the question. What's wrong?"

"My best friend kept me up half the night talking about himself, and eventually I found out that he thinks I'm disgusting, and I just found out that being a good listener apparently gets you nowhere," I said, "so all I did was make an ass of myself and waste my time all semester."

"Okay," I could see that Ken was trying not to laugh at me. "Since the semester is almost over, I can see why this is a problem. You could have said you don't want to talk about it. Want to go down for coffee after class and we can not talk about it some more? My treat?"

"I really don't want to talk about it," I warned him.

"We always have plenty of other things to talk about." He wasn't the least bit frightened by my scowl. "The whole point of the exercise is, you look like you need cheering up."

How could I not soften at that? "I guess I do. Thank you. I would very much like to go for coffee with you after class."

I kept stealing glances at him all the way through Spanish class. Had he just asked me on a first date? How had I overlooked him as a potential love interest?

I suppose because he's short. He must get overlooked a lot. He's not extremely short, but at most he's only an inch taller than me. Maybe we're the same height.

We ended up in different groups when the teacher divided the entire class in half to make conversation groups. I sat where I could see him. Light brown hair, blue eyes, the sort of lean but strong build you'd expect from a wrestler. Not that I knew much of anything about wrestling, but at least it fit in my imagination.

I smiled at him when class was over and we got back to our tables to collect our books. "¿Vamos a ir?"

"Sí. Vamos a tomar un café."

We talked in Spanish all the way to Starbucks. When I started ordering my Grande Skinny Caramel Macchiato in Spanish, the clerk stared at me across the counter, and Ken started laughing. "Try it again in English," he suggested.

"Oh. Yeah." I ordered again. A lot less staring occurred. Ken placed his order, we collected our beverages, and we found ourselves a wonderful little nook among the chairs and couches. This place has got to be the best library in the world. I know libraries are supposed to be about books, but they're also about quiet public places where you can study. Or talk to your friends. It's a place to be.

I kept expecting him to bring up my tragic sighs, and ask me again what's wrong. He never did. He talked about all sorts of other things, and kept me chatting and laughing until I completely forgot that I had just been told that dating me would be disgusting.

What was I thinking? Why did I think that eventually Eddie would come around and notice that there I was, faithfully waiting in the wings while he mooned over Katie?

The answer is simple. Jane Austen isn't the only one who has a story where friends (okay, in her case cousins) fall in love. Hollywood is full of stories where best friends make a pact to get married if they don't find anyone else by a certain age. Or where friends don't realize they've fallen in love until someone else comes along. Or... I don't know. But there are plenty of other stories where friends don't say it would be disgusting to start dating.

Ken walked me to my next class. "You look like you're feeling more cheerful. Keep it up." That was his only reference back to my troubles. Then he kissed my cheek, and walked away.

I don't think I heard a single word all the way through eastern philosophy class. All I could think about was that kiss on my cheek. That had been a date.

Dec 1

I have all these final papers due, but my dorm room is not the best place to get things done. You'd think the quiet would be great, but it's not. All I can see is the bed where I sat and found out that Eddie thought it would be disgusting to date me. I had so many text conversations with him while sitting at this desk.

I thought I would hole up in my room with carryout Chinese food and a package of Oreo cookies, and crank away at my projects. But the room was closing in on me. I needed a change of venue.

Fortunately, dorms are equipped with common rooms. I grabbed my laptop and books and headed down the hall.

I wasn't the only one who decided to find a different place to study. There were several people working away, all frowning and muttering. You can tell it's almost finals time.

Lon the floor nerd was there among the studious. He was sitting on one of the couches, leaning forward to type on his laptop. There was a girl on the couch next to him, but no one sitting on the couch across from them.

"May I join you?" I asked. I realized I could have plunked myself down without saying anything, but I felt the need to be more polite than that. I think I just needed the contact with other people.

Lon looked up from his laptop. "By all means."

While I was putting my books down on the coffee table between us, the girl sitting on the couch with Lon was looking me over.

"Hi," she greeted me. "What's your name?"

"I'm Lizzie," I introduced myself. "And you are?"

"Larissa," she answered. "It's nice to meet some of Lon's friends."

I didn't know what to say to that. I wasn't even sure if I counted as Lon's friend. But I didn't suppose I could tell her that. "Nice to be met." I didn't want to talk too much, people were here to study.

But Larissa kept up a steady chitchat with me while I was getting myself settled. Where am I from, how did I know Lon, what is my major. Finally I got her to shut up by picking up one of my books and holding it up in front of my face and starting to read. Then she only asked me two more questions, until Lon put his hand on her to quell her stream of questions. "She's trying to get her homework done, honey," he told her. "Leave her be."

He called her 'honey?' Well, in case it wasn't clear enough, Lon the floor nerd had a girlfriend. I smiled over at him to thank him for getting her to leave me alone. He gave me a nod in return, and then his attention went back to his laptop.

It was interesting, observing Lon and Larissa. They were a funny contrast. She was all bubbly and chatty and snuggly, and he was all quiet and prim and even a little standoffish, maybe. I couldn't quite put my finger on it. I felt a little sorry for Larissa, she obviously wanted to be making out, not sitting there studying. He obviously wanted to get some serious homework done, so I felt a little sorry for him, too. They had very different agendas tonight.

It was the funniest thing, but for some reason as I watched them over the top of my art history book, I was sorry I hadn't accepted when Lon asked me out last year.

Of course, that didn't matter, did it, if I was going to start dating Ken?

Dec 3

I've been expecting Ken to text me. We have each other's phone numbers, after all. But he hasn't. What's the etiquette on these things, anyway? Am I supposed to text him if he doesn't text me? Is that bad form? Fortunately, Spanish class meets Monday, Wednesday, and Friday, so I don't have to wait too long to see him again.

Today I got to class before he did. "Hey," I greeted him when he came in.

"Hey," he answered. "You're looking more cheerful today."

"And it seems to me you're looking less cheerful." He's a pretty chipper guy, but there was definitely a downward turn to his mouth. "Is it my turn to ask what's wrong?"

"Yeah, and my turn to say I don't want to talk about it."

"Okay, we'll see if I can do as good a job as you at cheering people up." I started singing to him in Spanish. We had to pick a Spanish-language pop star to write about for class, I wrote about Juanes. "Me Enamora" was the perfect song, edgy, yet a love song. And the line that means "love me with your mouth" is really hot.

He smiled a little, but I was a long way from making a difference. This girlfriend thing was going to be difficult, I could tell. I remembered Professor Jacobson's thing about finding the right formula. And then I didn't want to think about that anymore. I tried a different tactic. I settled for thinking that one date doesn't automatically make someone a girlfriend or boyfriend.

We actually sat at our tables for most of class. I was able to reach over and put doodles on his notes, and we played dots and boxes on mine. Then we did one of those games where one person starts a drawing with a single shape, and you take turns adding to it. We ended up with a funny looking ostrich-looking sort of creature.

So, maybe we didn't learn so much Spanish while we were there....

After class we went for coffee again. I offered to buy, since I was the one trying to cheer him up this time, but he insisted on paying again. And he walked me to my class again. And he kissed my cheek again. "Thank you, you really did cheer me up. You're a great friend."

A great friend? I don't know what to make of that. Is he being shy, not sure how to proceed with this dating thing? I certainly don't know much about the rules. I didn't really date in high school.

Mixed signals. While I sat down in my chair, I thought about Elinor Dashwood trying to figure out Edward Ferrars. I'm glad we don't live in a time of secret engagements and marriages that are all about money!

Today I was determined to pay more attention in ethics class. I didn't take a single note all through the lecture on Wednesday.

Dec 5

I couldn't stand it any longer. I had to text Ken over the weekend.

Hey

Hey

¿Qué Pasa?

No más. ¿Tu?

Just wondering how you're doing. Or if you're in need of coffee. I haven't gone for lunch yet.

Coffee isn't lunch.

It is sometimes.

How are you doing? Are
you in need of coffee?

I love how coffee has become a euphemism for moral support.

> I'm good. Just doing my homework
> while I'm sitting at my desk job.

Desk job?

> I work at the circulation desk for the
> law library.

Oh, yeah. I forgot.

> And, like I said, I haven't taken my
> lunch break yet.

I already ate. But thanks for
thinking of me.

> No charge.

I almost texted him later to see about getting dinner, but while I was walking home, Anne texted me and said she really needed me to go to a party with her. Since a frat party meant free food as well as free drinks, how could I say no to that? Especially since I hadn't seen her since my birthday.

It was actually a really good party. It had a Hawaiian theme, and everybody was wearing Hawaiian shirts or bathing suits, or grass skirts and coconut shells, or something. When you walked in the door, they put a lei around your neck. Over and over, the frat boys liked to point out that absolutely everyone got "laid" at their party. Ha ha.

They had a whole roasted pig, and mahi-mahi, and some goop called poi, and tons of fruit. Served in a carved-out pineapple, of course. They also had Mai Tais, and Hurricanes, and Blue Hawaiians, and Blue Lagoons, and Sex on the Beach, and all kinds of fruit daiquiris. And all kinds of different flavors of rum that were mixed with all sorts of different fruit juices.

A bunch of the guys who were wearing grass skirts got goaded into doing a hula - including Lon the floor nerd! Turns out this is his fraternity. It was pretty funny. I heard there was a hot tub out back, clothing optional, but I never went out to investigate. I'm sure there was a lot of pressure to opt out of the clothing, and I wasn't ready to strip for a tub full of frat boys. Even with several drinks in me, I wasn't so drunk that that sounded like a good idea.

I was in the dining room with a large group that was playing this board game that required cards and dice and a lot of answering questions, when Lon's girlfriend Larissa skipped into the room. She was laughing, and she was wearing a cowboy hat that was obviously too big for her.

Lon followed her into the room "Come on, Larissa, give it back."

I was surprised and a little amused. Lon owns a cowboy hat? It seems really out of character for him.

"But it looks so good on me," she protested. Wow, was she drunk. I've never seen anyone that wobbly, slurred-speech, won't-remember-a-thing-tomorrow drunk. She held up her hand, the one that was holding one of the blue drinks in it, and said "Lookit me, everybody, I'm a cowboy! Yeehaw!"

Lon winced. "Aw, please, Larissa, that's a Stetson you're sloshing your drink on. Give me back my hat."

"What'll you gimme in exchange?" she asked. I think she was trying to be sexy, but she was so drunk, it really wasn't.

"Anything you want, but please, let me have it back." I realized this was probably the most words I've ever heard out of him at one time. And the most worked up. He's usually pretty chill.

"Wow," I said to the person next to me at the table, "he must really like that hat."

The guy looked at me, and he had the same horror in his eyes that Lon had in his. "That's a Stetson. Do you understand how much a Stetson costs?"

I shrugged and shook my head. "It's a hat. How much can a hat cost?"

"Hundreds."

"Hundreds?" I gulped.

"Several hundreds. A really nice one can cost over a thousand dollars."

"I had no idea," I glanced over my shoulder at Larissa, still dancing around, the drink in one hand, and now the hat in the other. "I would be afraid to touch it."

Lon finally got his hat back. Larissa made some sort of noise of protest, then started laughing some more, and singing some song about no fences. "Hey, I know you," she said when she saw me. "You're his friend from the dorm. He told me he helped you with math last year, you aren't very good at calculus."

"Guilty," I admitted. I looked around the table at my fellow game players, then looked back at her. "Did you really have to 'out' me in a room full of engineers? Now they'll refuse to associate with me."

"That's okay, they won't remember if I get them all another drink," she laughed. She held up her glass, which was now empty. I wondered how much of it was in her, and how much was on Lon's hat. He was over by the lamp, looking at his hat with an expression that suggested that quite a bit of it had ended up on the hat. "Well, I need another drink, at least!" She reached out to show me her empty glass.

And that's when things got a little too exciting for a party. She tripped, and fell, and hit her head on the back of my chair on her way to the floor. The glass smashed to pieces. And that's when she started vomiting.

"Oh my God!" I was trapped between the table, the downed Larissa, the broken glass, and the vomit. Everyone jumped up, all talking at once, and running for stuff to clean up the glass, and to clean up the puke. Lon came over to get Larissa to sit up and at least use a trashcan to vomit into. She sat up, and that's when I saw the blood in her hair. "Oh, my God," I said again. "She's bleeding."

"It isn't too bad, is it?" someone asked.

Since I was the one in the chair right above her head, I had to look. I gingerly pulled her hair away from where the blood seemed to be coming from. "Oh, yeah, it's not good. She's going to need stitches in that. Someone better call an ambulance."

"We can't call an ambulance. She isn't 21, is she?"

I looked around. There were a lot of scared, uncertain faces. They weren't going to call for help. I pulled out my cell phone and dialed 911. "Hello? Hi. My name is Lizzie Barrett. My friend and I are on Campus Drive, and she just fell and split her head open. What's my friend's name?" I looked at Lon.

"Larissa Miller," he said softly.

"Larissa Miller," I repeated. We used the same trick to give the dispatcher the address, and some more information about Larissa.

"We'll be right there. Just stay calm," I was told.

"Is there anything I can do while I'm waiting for you? Ice or something?" I asked.

"Compression is good. Ice wouldn't hurt if you have some available."

I wanted to say, "Hey, this is a frat party, of course they've got ice." But of course I didn't. Instead, in an act of extreme grace, I dropped my phone and accidentally hung up on the dispatcher.

I thought about calling back, but I figured they'd be here any moment. I shoved my phone back in my pocket. "Can someone get me her purse?" I asked. I realized I didn't even have anything with me but my phone, my student ID, and my dorm card. For all I know she didn't have much more on her.

"Here it is," someone handed me a small red leather square with a whole lot of strap.

Lon and another frat brother got Larissa to her feet. "Should you be doing that?" I asked. "Isn't it safer to leave her where she is?"

"If you're waiting for them on the front porch, they won't be eyewitnesses to all the drinking we've been doing," Lon's frat brother told me as we walked to the front door. "Do you think you'll be able to look sober enough so they won't make you take a breathalyzer test?"

I looked at them. "I don't know. I don't suppose someone can get me a cup of coffee."

After we walked Larissa to the front porch and they sat her down, someone handed me a bag of ice. I tried to be gentle as I put it on top of her head, but she still cried out in protest. The frat brother ran off to get my coffee. Lon and I looked at each other.

"You don't mind staying with her?" he asked.

"Do you want to come, too?"

"I want to, but I shouldn't," he answered.

"Because your fraternity is implicated by giving alcohol to a minor? Because you could be in trouble for giving alcohol to a minor?" I guessed.

"Pretty much."

"Well, I'm a minor, too. I'll tell them she was drunk before we even came to your party. Problem is, when she wakes up, she'll contradict my story."

"No, I won't," she mumbled. Lon and I looked at each other.

"You'll tell them you were drunk before you got here?" he asked.

"I can do that," she mumbled.

"But then they'll ask you where you got the liquor from."

"I have a bottle of rum in my dorm room," she told us. "I don't need you guys to get a buzz."

"I see," he said. I could see he deplored this plan of action.

I had barely enough time to drink my cup of coffee before the paramedics showed up. "Hi, guys, sorry to bother you on such a lovely night," I said, trying to sound as laid-back and sober as I could. And it really was a pretty night. Not too cold, and the sky was really clear.

"What seems to be the trouble, here?"

"She fell and cracked her head open. These guys let us sit on the steps and brought us some ice. I wish I could stay, it sounds like a really fun party." I couldn't believe how cool I sounded to my own ears. I wondered what level of felony I'm committing by covering up illegal underage drinking. Is it a bigger crime to cover for someone else, or is it a bigger crime that I was drinking when I'm not 21?

The paramedics turned their full attention on Larissa, removing the ice pack, shining lights in her eyes to check her pupils. "Hey, that's not nice," Larissa protested.

"What's your name? "

"Larissa Miller."

"Where do you live?"

"Fulton House."

"What are you doing all the way down here?" the paramedic asked her.

"Walking. Or I was walking, then I was falling," she paused. "I think I might get sick again."

They held onto her while she threw up in the bushes.

"Feel better now? We're going to take you for a little ride, if you think you're ready."

"Oookay," she said.

While they walked her to the ambulance, I looked at Lon. "Thank you for your hospitality, I really appreciate it," I held out my hand. He shook it.

"Use her cell phone and call me when you can," he said softly. "Her phone passcode is 2826."

"I'll let you know how it goes," I promised him.

"I owe you."

"After the calculus help? I think we're even," I pointed out, then left to go get my first ride inside an ambulance. At least I wasn't the patient.

It was a long night. I'm so glad frat parties are on Saturdays. I didn't get home until about 4 am. When I walked in I flipped on the light, and Justine sat straight up in bed. "What's going on?" she shouted.

I quickly turned the light back off, and turned on the light in the closet so I could see while I undressed. "I'm so sorry, I didn't know you were going to be home tonight."

"John and I had a fight, I decided I'd rather stay here tonight," she explained. "Now what are you doing coming home at," she checked her phone, "four in the morning?"

"I just got out of the hospital," I explained, before I realized how bad that sounded.

"What were you doing in the hospital? And why didn't you call me, I would have come to pick you up."

"Oh, I wasn't the one who was sick. I went along with someone else who had an emergency while we were at a party."

"Is your friend okay now?"

"She's not really my friend, more a casual acquaintance. But yes, I think she's going to be fine."

"You spent the night in the hospital to take care of a casual acquaintance?" I'd turned off the light and crawled in bed, but I could tell from her voice that she was looking over at me incredulously.

"Yeah, I was in the wrong place at the wrong time," I explained.

"That was still above and beyond the call of duty. You're a really good person, Lizzie."

"I wish I felt like a good person," I admitted to her through yawns that were going to split my head open. "I feel kind of stupid, now that you make me look at things. She must have known someone else at the party, but here I was the one who went and spent the night helping her out."

"Because you're nicer. You're also more capable than lots of people. It's probably a good thing you were there, you know how to be responsible. I bet none of her friends were as good a choice to take care of her in a crisis."

"Wow." I thought of Anne Elliot in *Persuasion*, taking

charge after Louisa's accident at Lyme. Lon was like Captain Wentworth when he entrusted Katie to her care. I smiled into the darkness, thinking of Anne overhearing Captain Wentworth saying there was no one so proper, so capable as Anne. "Thanks, Justine."

"Sure. I'm going back to sleep now."

"Sweet dreams."

The last thing I did before I fell asleep was text Lon. I'd gotten his phone number earlier from Larissa's cell, when I'd called him to let him know what was going on when we got to the hospital.

> Larissa is home, I'm home. Bed now.

I didn't expect a response, but I got one immediately.

Thank you. You're one in a million. Sleep well.

> I plan to. You do the same.

I'll try.

Dec 12

I tried texting Ken tonight, but I never got much of a response. Just a "hey" when I said hello. It seems kind of weird, but since it's the start of finals, I guess it isn't that weird. When I didn't hear from him Monday or Tuesday, I knew it had to be because of finals. So I had to wait until our final on Wednesday to tell him about my adventures on Saturday night.

"You would not believe the weekend I had," I said as soon as I saw him.

"Hm," was all he said. It wasn't even a curious 'hm,' or a polite 'go-ahead, I'm listening' sort of 'hm.' It was more a distracted sort of 'hm.' So I went with the tell-him-anyway plan, as opposed to the get-upset-because-he's-not-listening plan.

"That's nice," he said when I stopped for air. Wow, talk about really not listening! Okay, time to do the listening, he must have a lot on his mind.

"Are you all right?" I asked.

"Sure, I'm fine," he answered.

"How was your weekend?"

"Good."

Wow, he wasn't giving me much to go on.

"That good, huh?" I prodded him. "No gory details? No tales of bravado and derring-do?"

"No, nothing that exciting. Got all my homework done. That can be a triumph of a sort. I had a big paper I had to turn in this morning. I'm really glad the biology final isn't until Friday."

"Well, then, you should look happier."

"Oh," he finally sighed and said, "I had a kind of unhappy conversation with my parents over the weekend. I want to be a marine biologist, but my parents don't think I'd make enough money living at a study facility on a beach in Costa Rica. My mother wants me to go to business school. My father wants me to get an accounting degree to go into banking or finance, and I think my grandmother wants me to be a CEO. I can't even just be an accountant, that still isn't good enough for them."

I was amazed. Did he sound like Edward Farris, or what? Well, I could certainly learn a thing or two from Elinor Dashwood. She was certainly the more admirable sister, if you think about it. Kind and selfless and steady. What would Elinor say?

"What are you going to do?"

"I don't know. It's my life, I should be able to do what I want. But they're the ones paying for my education. So I'm kind of stuck."

"Can you take out student loans? Or, can you get your MBA, and then use the money from being a CEO to fund your marine biologist degree?" I asked.

Ken smiled a little. "I will admit, that hadn't occurred to me."

The teacher started handing out the exam books for the final. I was so glad I was able to get a smile out of him, at least, beforehand. Then the lights went out, and we watched a short movie, after which we had to answer a lot of questions about it.

After class, I took him by the elbow and started steering him toward coffee. "I was falling asleep during that movie, I bet you were, too, and I got paid today. So I insist it's my turn to pay for coffee."

Ken gave a soft little snort. "If I choose to be a poor marine biologist, I should never turn down an offer if someone else is buying. Of course, if I do what Mommy and Daddy tell me, someday I'll be able to buy vats of coffee, and I'll never need to accept an offer from a lady."

This was going to be tough. "That's for Future Ken to worry about. And I hope in either case Future Ken will not be a chauvinist, and either one of you would accept when a lady offers to buy you a cup of coffee." I figured this line of thinking wasn't going to help him with his problem much. The best thing I could do for him was to keep asking questions. "What would make you happier? Studying fish, or pleasing your parents?" Wow, the coffee line was long. Fortunately, it always moved quickly.

My question brought out another soft little snort, but there was sort of a smile with it, so I'm going to count that as a win. "There are all sorts of marine life that aren't fish," he pointed out.

"Okay, fine, what would make you happier, studying eels and mollusks and dolphins and sharks and whales and sea otters, or pleasing your parents?" I re-asked the question, and then I had to wait for the answer because we had to place our order.

"I've never had to choose before," he answered.

"Would you really be in that much trouble if you don't go to business school?" I asked.

"Well, I'm in trouble if I declare my biology major," he explained. "Almost the same thing."

"Can you double major?" I was trying to see a way around this predicament.

"Not much in the way of overlapping credits," he said, but I could see he was thinking about it.

"You could end up being an accountant for Greenpeace," I suggested.

He smiled for real at that. "My parents would really hate that. Those people are probably not making the same kind of money as Wall Street executives or bank presidents."

They handed us our coffees, and we strolled away. We sort of meandered around campus, sipping our coffees, and looking for answers.

"What if you can't get in to business school?" I realized.

"What do you mean?"

"Well, even though it would be kind of a waste taking all the accounting prerequisites, you could make sure you bombed the GMAT." I was getting excited about this idea. "If you take the test and can tell what the right answers are, pick a wrong answer. They won't take you in business school if your GMAT scores are wretched, right?"

Ken stopped walking and thought about that for a minute. Then his face fell. "You might have something, there, but you don't know my parents. They would probably go and interview all my professors to find out why I failed. Or they'd go to the dean of the school and demand that all the professors get fired because I wasn't getting the tools I needed to succeed. Or they'd blame the testing service and sue them. I don't want to be the reason a bunch of honest people get fired."

"Boy!" I was running out of ideas. "They really have every angle covered, don't they?"

"So I have a choice to make. Do what I want, and become a poor orphan, or do what they want, and become a poor rich boy with a career I despise."

I stared at him, thinking of my erstwhile career as a pharmacist. My parents had fussed about my major, but they didn't try to force me to do something I'd hate. "I got nothin," I shook my head. "This sounds awful, but I don't envy you."

We were standing in front of my building. I knew I was late for my next exam, but I didn't care. I would have stood there forever, or, at least as long as Edward, I mean Ken, needed me.

He was late for his exam, too, and he obviously didn't care, either. "I don't envy me, either. This Christmas break is gonna suck." He leaned forward and kissed me on the forehead this time. Long and fervently. Then he wrapped his arms around me and gave me a giant hug. "Thank you, Lizzie. You're a really, really great friend." He held me for a long while, rocking back and forth a little. Then he let go. "We're insanely late. Talk to you later?"

"Text me if you want to talk more later," I told him.

My heart was pounding so hard I could hear it clearly in my ears. I was sorry that he was going through this, but at the same time, I was so happy, I could have danced down the hall.

Dec 15

Anne talked me into going with her and a few of her sorority sisters to a horror movie tonight, since we'd all finished our finals. This is SO not me. I'm just not into horror movies.

But, they had free movie passes, someone couldn't go at the last minute, I was available, and Anne wouldn't take no for an answer. Okay, fine, I'll go and be sociable. I hadn't seen her since the disastrous frat party that ended up with me going to the hospital with Lon's girlfriend.

We all grabbed dinner at the place that sells the giant bowls of noodle soup and an egg roll for $5.99, then we got to the theatre early enough to get drinks and candy bars or popcorn, and settle into the best seats – the ones in the exact center of the theatre.

I hadn't met most of this batch of Anne's sorority sisters. They were all pretty nice, but sort of the same girl, over and over. I was glad I decided not to pledge. I don't wear enough makeup nor wear high heels just to go sit in the dark and watch a movie. Not that I go to that many movies, but there it is.

Brittany is the only one I'd met before, at one of the parties last year. She's the brassiest one in the group. I can easily imagine her being a trial lawyer. She's very bold, direct, and outspoken. She also has a raunchy sense of humor: it might get in the way of a successful law career. I bet juries frown on dirty jokes.

Jen is the ringleader, if I had to guess. She is about to graduate with a Physical Therapy degree, and she's always correcting people. "Put your shoulders down. Don't stand like that. Have you been doing your crunches? Yeah, I can tell you haven't been." She's bossy, but she's right. When I stooped down to pick up my ticket after I dropped it, she gasped "Don't do that! Don't have your knees going out past your toes like that! That's terrible form." I vaguely remembered my high school gym teacher saying something about keeping knees over your feet.

Bunny is a cute little quiet one who is all eyes with silky long blonde hair, and I think every guy who came near us hit on her: the server who took our order at the restaurant, the waiter who brought us our soup, the usher who took our tickets, and every guy at the concession stand where we bought our sodas. Must be rough.

Karla is the sexpot. Big eyes, high pitched voice, another raunchy sense of humor. She is the one most likely to grab the boobs of the other girls. They are all very handsy, and obviously close, but if there is horsing around and body parts are getting grabbed, she is most likely the instigator.

I was a little amazed when Karla insisted on sitting next to me when we got to our seats. "I get to mess with the new girl!" she claimed.

Once we were seated, she pulled out a flask, and took the lid off her cup to pour some in with her soda. Then she handed the flask to me. "Take some, pass it down," she said. "There should be enough for everybody."

"What is it?" I asked. I took a sniff. It smelled like almonds and vanilla.

"Rum," she explained as I was figuring that out from the smell. "What's a horror movie without a rum and coke to go with it?"

"I see," I said. Now I understood why everyone told me to get Coke instead of Mountain Dew. I also guessed that was another reason why they liked to get to the show a little on the early side.

While the flask was getting passed down the line, Karla took a sip of hers and looked me over. "So, it's about time I've met you. I swear, everyone I know already knows you."

"Everyone?" I raised my eyebrows with some skepticism.

"Anne always talks about you, of course, and the editor I used to be on yearbook staff with in high school, Darcy, says he knows you. Even my calculus professor found a hair tie that you left in his office after you went to get some help with your assignments. And then you know my boyfriend, Ken. He must talk about you more than anyone else."

A giant boulder magically materialized inside my stomach. "Your boyfriend Ken? Who would that be?"

"Ken Garvin. You're in Spanish class with him, aren't you? He says you are his best friend in the world, and I've been on his case for months for me to meet you. Problem is, I'm always either working or in class or asleep, so it seems like we hardly ever get to see each other. You'll notice even now I'm here, instead of with him. It's my first social outing in forever, and he insisted I should come. I offered to make him dinner tonight, since he's so upset about his conversation with his parents. But he said I should come out with the girls, and he was going to go do some nice, manly sulking by himself for a while."

I stared at her. Yeah, it sure sounded like the same Ken. I couldn't believe it.

"Don't look at me like that, you're making me feel guilty. You would have blown off the girlfriends, and been with your man in his hour of need, wouldn't you?" She squeezed my arm anxiously. "I tried to talk him into dinner with me, I swear I did. But I don't want to be some sort of clinging vine. If he says he wants some alone time, I'll give him some alone time. We both think it's healthy, having a big circle of friends, and we don't feel like we have to do everything together. We work out together, and study together, and eat together, but I insist he goes out with the guys sometimes, and he insists I go out with the girls sometimes. He's the sweetest guy in the world!"

I couldn't take the way her eyes were shining while she talked about him. He couldn't possibly feel about her the way she felt about him. Then I remembered Edward. He was engaged to Lucy when he wasn't in love with her anymore. That was it. Ken was in love with me, that's why he didn't want Karla coming over to make dinner for him. "Yes, he is a great guy," was all I said out loud.

I was very glad when the previews started, and she stopped talking to me.

Dec 16

I was really glad for the rum and cokes. Ironically, it was Karla's rum that got me pretty wasted that night. Talk about needing a drink.

So I have something of a hangover today. With nothing better to do, I decided to go find Ken after his biology exam this morning. I didn't know exactly where his exam was, but I knew which building it was in, and the door he probably would be coming out. I lurked on a nearby bench, trying to look casual, scanning faces as they came out the door.

There was a trickle of people, then a flood of people, then a trickle again. About to give up, I was figuring I'd missed him in the crowd, or he'd gone out a different door, or I was wrong about his exam schedule, when he walked through the doors.

Once I was watching him come down the stairs, I had no idea what to say to him. I lifted my sunglasses so he could see it was me. "Hey, I know you," I used for an opening line. Gotta play it cool for starters.

"Hey, I know you, too," he came over smiling and sat beside me on the bench. "What are you doing over here?"

Shit, now I was going to have to think of something. What business did a philosophy major have on the science half of the campus? And why would I be sitting outside on a cold bench on a December afternoon? "I had to pick up a prescription at the pharmacy before I left for home," I said, waving in the general direction of University Hospital. "And here I am walking back, and my hangover got the better of me. Sitting down for a minute seemed like a good idea."

"Well, it's a great idea, if it means I get to see you," he answered gallantly. "What a pleasant surprise, even if I'm sorry it's for an unpleasant reason."

Yeah, there was no way he was still in love with his girlfriend.

"Well, it was pleasant enough when I was giving myself this hangover in the first place," I decided to jump into the deep end of the pool. "I was out at the movies last night, and I got to meet your girlfriend Karla."

I watched him intently behind my sunglasses. Now I understand the expression 'hanging on his next words.' The next thing he said was going to seal my fate, somehow. I knew it.

"You did? That's terrific!" Ken was all smiles and enthusiasm. "Isn't she amazing? I'm so glad I talked her into going out with her girlfriends last night. She was going to come over and be a good supportive girlfriend, but I told her it would be better if I didn't have to play well with others. Even her. She might as well go have fun, I needed to do some thinking that required alone time. I know she would have brought over something to do and just been with me, silently, if I wanted the moral support, but I figured I'm not six years old. I don't need someone to hold my hand. So what did you think of her? Isn't she the sweetest girl in the world?"

I was speechless. I had to think of something to say. What would Elinor say? "Why, yes, she is very sweet. And generous." I put my hand to my aching head. "Maybe a little too generous. With her rum, at least."

"She does love her rum," Ken said with a heartbreakingly intimate smile. "Smuggled it in her water bottle again, did she?"

"No, it was an actual flask," I told him.

"She keeps getting better at smuggling. I keep telling her someday she'll be smuggling guns or something else illegal that will get her in so much trouble, they'll make a Hollywood movie based on her life."

I needed him to stop talking about how wonderful she was. Maybe walking would change the direction of the conversation. "I think I'm ready to continue. Shall we?" I stood up. And then wobbled a little. "Whoa."

He stood up, too, and took my arm in concern. "Are you sure you're okay? Why don't you sit back down?"

I didn't want to sit there anymore. "No, I think I'd rather tough it out and get back to my dorm."

"As you wish." I looked at him quickly, thinking of The Princess Bride. But no, I think he was only being considerate.

As we walked along, he got back to the topic of his girlfriend. "I'll have to chastise her for getting you too drunk. You're obviously not as used to this much liquor."

"I hold my own most of the time," I defended myself.

"She's insane. Talk about a wooden leg. She can drink most people under the table, and she never gets a hangover. I think she must have a seriously impressive metabolism."

How am I supposed to compete with that? I don't know what my metabolism is like. "That's really something," I said vaguely.

Unfortunately, he took that as encouragement to talk about her some more. "I told her some of the things you'd said about my options. You know, do I make myself happy, or do I make my parents happy. She said you were really insightful to put it that way."

"Glad I could be of service," I didn't want her praising me. But I couldn't tell him that.

"She and I decided that I'm going to stand my ground and make my own career choice. If I let them manage my life now, they will be managing my life until they die. I don't want to wait that long to start living my life. We're probably going to get an apartment together off campus next year if my parents cut me off. She pointed out that at least this year, my dorm and tuition are paid for, so I'm not getting kicked out of school even if they won't pay for any more of my college."

He threw an arm around my shoulders and gave me a squeeze as we walked up to my dorm. "Thank you so much for helping me work through this. You and Karla have got to be the two best women a man can have in his life."

I tried to smile. "No charge." I kissed him on the cheek, this time, and walked as nonchalantly as I could into the building. I wanted to run away. I was going to break down in tears, and I couldn't exactly do that in front of him. I was never so glad to own sunglasses before.

This is not how it's supposed to work out! Didn't he read the script? This is where he's supposed to tell me that he's been dating her for five years, and it's pretty much stale, and since they never see each other, they've been drifting apart, and besides, he met me.

Karla didn't read the script either. She's supposed to abandon him at the prospect of him being cut off from his family's money, and transfer her affections to his younger brother.

Lon the floor nerd was waiting for the elevator when I stepped out of it. Which was awkward, since the first thing I did the moment the doors opened was rush out, and I crashed straight into him. "Watch out," he said, catching me after I crashed straight into his chest. I never noticed before how tall he is! He set me back on my feet. "You're like a cannonball on a mission."

"Yeah. Sorry!" I wished he'd take his hands off my arms and get out of my way. At the same time I didn't want him to. "I'm in kind of a hurry."

"I gathered that much. Well, then, I won't detain you." He stepped aside and gave a courtly nod.

I ran down the hall, confused, my heart fluttering a little from his gentlemanly gesture, while I still needed to have a good cry over Ken.

Dec 20

Christmas break is such a relief. I don't have to face Ken for several weeks, although he'll probably be in my Spanish class next semester. Maybe I'll text him and ask which section he's in, and I'll arrange my schedule so that I'm in a different class. That's probably a good strategy. But I'm not texting him today.

The first thing I did when I got home was sit down and play two hours of video games with my little brother. Blowing things up can be incredibly therapeutic. It's a little amazing that David was willing to play with me so long. I was beating the pants off him game after game. He finally quit on me.

"Wow, you must have had a really lousy time at school, or you're really mad at someone," he threw his controls onto the coffee table. "You never play like this. I've never seen you shoot so fast. Who do think you're shooting at?"

"Actually, the correct grammar would be 'at whom do you think you're shooting,'" I told him. "But that's me being a dick. Thanks for noticing. There was a guy at school I was really interested in, but it turns out he already had a girlfriend."

"That stinks," David said. Then he blinked. "Wait, I thought Wendy said you were going out with Eddie Jameson?"

"I wanted to, but it didn't work out."

"Why didn't it work out? You've been best friends for so long, it makes sense." He had such a puzzled frown on his face, I reached over and hugged him.

"It just didn't. It's kind of embarrassing. He was interested in another girl for a while, and then that didn't work out, and I thought for sure we'd get together. I was being his best friend, and a good listener, and he told me he could tell me anything. But when I suggested we could try dating, he said that was gross, he couldn't do that."

"Well, that's weird and illogical." David has just discovered the existence of Star Trek, and he's now a big Spock fan.

"I thought so, too. That's what makes *Mansfield Park* so believable. It's logical that Edmund eventually wakes up and gives his heart to Fanny."

"Jane Austen again. There's your real problem." In one sentence David transformed from a sympathetic listener back into my little brother. "Why do you want to be a character from a Jane

Austen book, anyway? All the characters do is worry about marrying rich guys. You're not gonna marry a rich guy, you're in college so you can get a good job and never have to get married at all."

"You don't get it," I tried to explain. "Jane Austen's heroines always have admirable qualities, and there's always a happy ending."

"Real life doesn't have happy endings," he told me with perfect 11-year-old logic. "Real life keeps on going, until you die, and that's never a happy ending. Unless you're like, really sick and in pain and death is better than living with all the pain."

All I could do was laugh.

Dec 27

I worked up the nerve to text Ken to say Merry Christmas, and asked when he was taking Spanish. He told me, and now I'm working on getting my schedule fixed so that I have to take something else during his class.

Mom came in while I was online, working on my class schedule, and started reading over my shoulder. "What's this?"

"I'm figuring out my class schedule," I told her.

She peered at the screen. "These are your classes? Ethics? Logic? The Philosophy of Love and Sex?"

"These are all important things to think about, Mom," I told her.

"You're not taking any science courses at all? This is all just fluff."

I turned around in my chair. "I suck at science, Mom. I bombed all my science classes, you know that."

"You did alright in calculus."

"Only because I was practically sleeping with the professor." I didn't need to tell her the whole sordid story. That summary was close enough. "Your daughter is not a science person. I'm no good at it."

My mother was just kind of staring wide eyed at me, so I went on. "I brought up my GPA this semester by taking a bunch of philosophy classes. It's a subject I enjoy. I got A's instead of C's and F's. Medicine requires ethics, I can do something at the nursing home that uses an ethics degree."

"We don't have any employees at the nursing home who majored in philosophy," she told me sharply. "People need a practical education, not a lot of hooha talking about Plato and Aristotle."

"Well, maybe that says something bad about the medical field," I responded equally sharply. "Who is asking the important questions, then? Who takes care of a patient's rights? Who defends a doctor when patients refuse treatment, and then they blame the doctor when they get sicker?" I thought about my job at the law library. Oh god, I was going to end up in law school like Darcy. Ew! I'd better find a different argument, quickly. "Education needs to spend more time on critical thinking skills, and less time on job training."

"So you're planning on getting out of school with an education, but no skills that make you employable?" Mom asked bitterly. "This is not what we're sending you to school for."

"Just because you won't employ me, doesn't mean nobody will give me a job," I answered.

My mother glared at me. "Tell you what, you like being on the computer, you go find some jobs that are hiring people with philosophy degrees. You show me what jobs you'll be qualified to do when you get out of school. Show me who is going to pay you money, so that you can pay for your rent, and a new car, and all the other things you're going to need money for when you graduate and start your first real job."

I glared back at her. "Fine, I will."

Dec 28

I spent several hours this morning looking all over the internet, and I have to concede Mom's right. Unless I go to law school, there's really not much of anything I can do with a degree in philosophy. Except maybe be a really entertaining waitress. I could ask my tables philosophical questions when they place their orders. But that could hurt my tips, since some people find questions uncomfortable.

So now what do I do? I want to talk to Ken about all of this so badly. He would understand my predicament. Sort of. At least he has a career in mind. I don't want to do what my parents want me to do. Their career choice would be disastrous for me. But what should I do instead?

At least I've come to one conclusion. A college education doesn't actually prepare you for real world jobs.

So I had another talk with my parents. I told them about my job search, and that I didn't think I really wanted to go to law school, which was the only way I could think of to turn a philosophy degree into a paycheck.

"The last thing the world needs is more lawyers," my father grunted. "I'm glad you don't want to be a lawyer."

"So what are you going to study?" my mom asked me.

I looked at them miserably. "I'm not sure. Can I go take a bunch of different classes, and try to find out what I'm good at? I've got to be good at something."

I sounded so pathetic, I must have melted my parents' hearts. They both started crying, and hugging me, and reassuring me that there was something out there that I would be able to do. They told me I was good at lots of things, and reminded me that I always got straight A's in high school. I'm not sure that counts for anything in college, but at least it's nice to know that once upon a time, I was smart.

So, this semester I'm going to take an intro to business class, and a class that is an intro to marketing, and a class about teaching exercise classes at a gym, or a rec center, or something. There is also a class on hospitality management. Running a nursing home might not be all that different than running a hotel. Could be fun, right? I've also got a photography course. It might be cool to work for a newspaper taking pictures. Of course David says it would be so much cooler if there really were superheroes, and I could be chasing down Superman, or Spiderman, or something. And Wendy thinks I should take photography in order to become a photographer who shoots fashion models.

Maybe this isn't so bad. And of course I'm also taking Spanish. Got to do something that's just for fun.

Feb 6

The rest of Christmas break was rejuvenating. My brother and sister and I played a lot of video games, and argued (that was mostly my sister, and mostly about clothes), and partied with my parents' friends from college on New Year's Eve. My dad went to college with three friends, and they've stayed in touch all these years. The parents decided to hang out for New Year's, and they invited all of us kids (if you can call us all kids. Michael Knox is something like 17 years older than me). It turned into something like a family reunion. Almost all of us were able to make it. We ate, we drank, we talked, we danced, we watched the ball drop on Times Square at midnight, and we played board games and card games until 3:00 in the morning. I beat Michael several times, which was satisfying. He's a bossy know-it-all who really likes to win. He hates being in second place.

The one thing I didn't do was get together with Eddie Jameson. We were both home from school, so we could have hung out, but I didn't want to. And he never tried to get ahold of me, so I guess it's mutual.

So now I'm back at school feeling refreshed and ready to face down last semester's love problems, while taking on my new class load of future possibilities. Sadly, I have to do it without the occasional use of Justine's car. "John's neighbor got rid of his car, so we get his parking space," she told me when I moved back in.

Regardless of the changes, some things remain constant, like Starbucks, and the "sweet" spot in the library. When I got out of hotel management class with a boatload of reading to do, I figured I'd better fortify myself with a caramel latte before I met up with Allie for some studying.

148

The barrista who handed me my coffee looked around. "Where's your friend today?"

"I haven't seen him since I got back to school." I knew he was talking about Ken, since we came here so often last semester.

"You guys have a fight?" he asked.

"Not really. I just… it's complicated. Maybe the easiest thing to say is, I don't like his girlfriend that much."

"Oh. I thought you were his girlfriend."

"I kind of thought so, too."

"I see. You did say it was complicated." His manager came over, and I thought he was in trouble for talking to me. Instead, she said, "Are you going to introduce me to your friend? I'm bored, too."

"Oh! Sorry, Michelle. This is…" he looked at me.

"Lizzie Barrett. Hi. He makes a really perfect caramel latte."

"Who, Nathan? Yes, he does. Would you like a little more caramel syrup on the top of yours? I've got a tiny bit left, I'd like to open a new one before the rush starts in a couple of minutes."

"Far be it from me to turn down extra caramel!" I held my cup out.

Nathan was checking out my sleeves. "Wow, that is really some shirt. Those are great sleeves."

I love this shirt. It has long circular ruffles that go almost from wrist to elbow. I feel like the heroine in a romance novel whenever I wear it. "Thanks. I got this at the thrift store last year.

It's one of my favorite tops."

"No kidding? Everything I'm wearing today came from the thrift store."

"No way! I didn't know guys do thrift stores." I remembered Darcy Fitzwilliam's crack about my not going out with him while wearing a dress I found at the thrift store. Nathan was certainly a vast improvement.

"They do sell men's clothes. Of course, there's always a lot less to pick from. But the same thing's true if you go to a shopping mall. Guys are supposed to wear less, I guess."

I opened my mouth, shut it, and buried my face into my coffee cup. I didn't know this guy well enough to say something salacious.

I was saved by the arrival of more customers. No doubt this was the rush his boss was talking about. "I'll see you around, Nathan," I toasted him with my cup.

"Hey, before you go, I don't have your number," he told me.

That has got to be the cheekiest request for a phone number, ever! And I've heard some good lines at the frat and sorority parties. I handed him my cup. "Since you're the one with the marker, write your number on mine, and I'll text you," I suggested.

"That works." He scribbled it onto the side of my cup. "Talk to you later."

I took my cup back. He'd written, "Text me soon," and his phone number.

"I will," I promised. He grinned at me, and went back to making coffees.

As much as I wanted to go around the corner and text "I miss you already," I thought maybe that would come across as too desperate. So I waited a couple of hours before I texted, "Hey, this is Lizzie. Now you have my number, too."

Maybe he was trying not to seem desperate, himself, because it was two hours before he texted back, "Sweet."

Feb 8

Okay, this texting thing with a guy I've just met is tricky. For two days now, I've been trying to think of something to say to Nathan. I've polled everyone. Justine and John thought I should abandon the idea of texting him, and go see him at the coffee shop. I tried that a couple of times, but he hasn't been working at the times I stopped by. Then Allie and her mom told me I should text him to say I went to see him. But Tiffany told me not to do that, it makes me sound desperate.

Well, what if I am desperate? I feel like I've gone from one guy to the other, one romantic possibility to another, and there's always so much potential, but then nothing comes of it. I know my brother keeps telling me I shouldn't expect real life to be like a Jane Austen novel. But so many times, I seem to come so close! Is it too much to ask of life, to find a gentleman with a romantic streak?

Instead of getting my marketing reading done, I sat on my bed with all of Jane's books, and scanned through them. Were her heroes actually romantic? When Edmund chases Mary Crawford, lets face it, it's just lust. He's thinking with his dick. But in the end, I think he is a romantic. That's why Fanny loves him.

Colonel Brandon is definitely a guy with a romantic streak. He stays true to his dead love for so long. And then, when he meets Marianne, his devotion to her is so deep.

Does it make him less of a romantic that he loves Marianne because she reminds him of the lost love? I hadn't thought about that before. Maybe that's a little less flattering. I'll say that it only accounts for his first attraction to her.

Mr. Darcy, is he a romantic? He seems all business. But then he does so much for the Bennett family, and doesn't even want them to know, he's doing it all because he's in love with Lizzie. That's about as romantic as it gets.

So, is Nathan romantic? If he's not, can I live with that? He likes thrift stores, maybe that's more pragmatic than romantic. He's friendly. Well, he seems friendly, even though he hasn't texted me anything else after his one-word reply. I guess it's too early to tell. All I can do is wait and see what happens.

Feb 16

Nathan finally texted me today. It's only been a week…

Are you on campus?

Yeah, are you?

Of course. I don't suppose you'd want to stop by the

coffee   shop?   There's
someone I want you to
meet.

Okay, that seemed kind of…forward. If there is such a word in this day and age. But it did pique my curiosity.

Will you be there when I get out of class in an hour?

Yep

That worked for me. Class was accounting, which was not far from the coffee shop. It's turning out to be kind of a dry topic, or maybe it's just a dry teacher, but I was very glad when class ended. I thought maybe business math would be better than regular math. I seem to be understanding it better, since it's about real dollars instead of imaginary numbers, but I'm already starting to think that I'm not going to become a business major. Wrong kind of checks and balances to be interesting. I practically ran out the door when class was over.

Nathan was watching for me. He waved me over when I approached the line to get coffee. "Hey, Lizzie."

I walked over to the counter where you pick up your order. "Hey, Nathan."

He grinned at me while finishing the order he was working on. "Glad you were able to pop by."

"My class is right around the corner, it's easy to do," I said. "Of course this building is probably exactly in the middle of campus, so you're not too far from anything."

An absolutely gorgeous girl who was also working behind the counter walked up next to Nathan and put her arm around him. "Is this her?" his coworker asked.

I wasn't sure I liked the way she was sizing me up. "That depends upon who 'her' is, and what you want from her," I was looking her over, too.

"What I want is to introduce you," Nathan said. "Natalie, this is Lizzie. Lizzie, this is my twin sister Natalie."

Natalie was pretty. Really pretty. Really, really pretty. I've never been so happy in my life to find out that someone was a sister. There was no competing with someone with Natalie's looks. "Hi! It's great to meet you," I said.

"You, too. Nathan's been telling me about you," she said.

"I'm not sure what there is to tell," I said, feeling a little sheepish. I mean, really, what was there to say? I gave him my phone number, I'd been waiting for him to text me something more than one word.

"He said you like thrift stores. We're going to make a run over to Goodwill tomorrow, want to join us?" Natalie asked.

"Goodwill? Isn't that kind of far away?" I couldn't think of one close to campus. There's a Salvation Army, and a St. Vincent de Paul, and a couple other quirky little second hand places.

"I have a car. Meet us in front of the student union, and I'll pick you and Nathan up?"

"That would be awesome!" I smiled at the both of them. I was going to ask if we wanted to go out to dinner while we were off campus, but then our conversation got cut short.

Their boss, Michelle, was having an increasingly heated conversation with some man in a suit. She was really looking steamed. "Yeah? Well, you know what? You can do me a big favor and drop dead."

"Not until after you get me my coffee," the man in the suit answered. He was obviously just as angry as Michelle was.

Michelle banged around behind the counter, moved a bunch of cleaning supplies out of her way, then sloshed coffee and milk and whatever else she was putting in his cup. She slammed on a lid, and slammed the cup on the counter. "There. Now get the fuck out of my shop," she told him curtly.

"Gladly."

She stood there a moment, gripping the counter, after he left. Then she realized that we were all staring at her. She twitched her shoulders a little and smiled at us. "Don't you love dealing with ex-boyfriends," she said with a laugh that had sort of a funny high pitch to it. Like a touch of hysteria.

"Yeah, my ex-boyfriends always seem to keep coming back to me, expecting me to feed them," Natalie said with a toss of her gorgeous hair.

I didn't know what to say, I've never officially had a boyfriend before.

"I never see either of my ex-girlfriends," Nathan said. "If we don't like each other well enough to date anymore, we don't like each other enough to seek out each other's company."

"I wish he had as much tact," Michelle said. "What a jackass." She took a deep breath, sort of gave herself a shake, and then smiled at me. "Hello again, Lizzie. Here for your caramel latte? I'll get it for you."

"That's okay, I can," Nathan offered to do it.

"It's on the house if you don't mind my using one of these cups I've dumped on the counter. They're still clean, I promise."

"I don't care," I said. "And I don't mind paying for it."

"Meh. Consider it a bribe. I'm buying your silence. I give you coffee, you pretend you did not witness that display of unprofessional behavior." She gave me her recomposed smile.

"Deal." I wasn't about to argue with free coffee. "I did not hear you swearing at all. There was no one here. Actually, I wasn't even here. I was in another part of the library."

Michelle smiled conspiratorily at me and handed me a cup. Extra whipped cream, and a ton of caramel drizzled on top. "Here you go."

I took a sip. "Yum. You might be even better at making these than Nathan."

"Well, I should be. After all, I'm the boss." Michelle was back to normal.

"Well, thank you boss." I looked at Nathan and Natalie. "I should get to class. See you tomorrow – what time are you going? We didn't actually say."

"We were planning on 4:00," Natalie answered. "Does that work for you?"

"Yeah, I think that should work."

"Okay, we'll see you tomorrow," Nathan smiled at me in a way that made me all happy and squishy inside. It lasted at least a couple of hours, I think.

Feb 17

I decided to do my studying in the student union, so that all I'd have to do is collect my stuff and go outside when it gets close to 4:00. I made myself a nice little nest in one of the quiet areas. I grabbed a comfy chair and one of the multipurpose ottomans that are scattered around among the chairs. I could use the ottoman as a table while I rummaged in my book bag, or I could use it to prop up my feet, or I could entertain visitors if any of my friends happened to pass through.

The friend that found me there was a complete surprise. Michael Knox is the oldest one of the kids produced by my parents' friends from college. Since we've known each other all our lives, he's kind of like having an extra sibling, or cousin, or something.

He was strolling through the student union. I happened to look up at the right time, and recognized him. "Michael?"

"Hi, Lizzie! I was about to call you."

"What are you doing here?" He's a lot older than me, so he's not the sort of person one would expect to be strolling through the student union.

"My firm is hopefully going to be doing some renovations here next year. I had to deliver the blueprints and budget estimates and go over our bid with the president and the trustees." Michael was an architect, or something like that. He owns a design firm.

"You're not going to do anything really modern and ugly, are you?" I asked.

"I am not one of those architects who would put a glass and steel front on a stone gothic church, no."

"Well, you like the glass pyramid in the middle of the Louvre, so there's never any telling with you."

"It's an art museum. It's modern art. It also lets in a lot of light, and it's a very attractive structure in its own right. It stands on its own merits." He sat down on the ottoman. "You will be reassured to know there will be no glass on the changes we're doing."

"That is reassuring."

"To make sure you are sincerely reassured, come on, I'll buy you an ice cream cone."

"You make me sound like a six-year-old."

"Well, then, don't pout like a six-year-old. Gather up your books and let's go. Unless you really don't have time for me right now. I can leave you to your studying, and I'll see you later."

"There's no way I will ever pass up an opportunity for ice cream, and you know it. Give me a second." I crammed my books into my book bag, and we set off for the ice cream shop, which is on the second floor.

Even though we had seen each other New Year's Eve, we hadn't actually talked that night. There were a lot of people there. Now that it was one on one, we had the chance to visit. We both had family gossip to share, and personal news we hadn't talked about at the party. Fortunately, we each got two scoops of ice cream.

"Well, I'd better get back to the office. This was fun. I'll let you know if I'm going to be back on campus anytime soon."

"Sure. You can always buy me ice cream. Or lunch. Or dinner."

He laughed as he hugged and kissed me goodbye. "You always were a shameless opportunist. I'll see you later, Beth. I mean, Liz? Is that what you're going by these days?"

"It's Lizzie. I am not an opportunist. That suggests both a ruthlessness and a set of organizational skills I know I don't possess. But thanks for the ice cream, Michael."

After he left, I wondered where I ought to go study. I could stay where I was at the little table. Although now I sort of wanted some coffee.

Coffee! I pulled out my phone to see what time it was. 4:47. Shit!

I grabbed all my stuff and ran through the union. Oh, shit, shit, shit. How could I have not noticed how late it was getting?

Michael. He could give me a lift over to the Goodwill. I pulled out my phone again and called him up.

No answer. He was probably driving, and he's very conscientious about never using his cell phone while driving. I think he's a little too anal about not using the phone – that's why they make hands-free things like earpieces so you can talk while you drive. But he lets his calls ring through to his voice mail, and answers them later.

Speaking of which, I got his voice mail. Since he wouldn't get my message until he was all the way back to his firm, there wasn't any point in my leaving him one. I hung up.

I realized there were three Goodwills in town, and I didn't know which one Nathan and Natalie were going to, anyway. I texted Nathan.

Hey! I'm sorry, I got derailed. Which Goodwill store are you at? I'm free now, I'll figure out how to join you, if you're still there.

I paced in front of the union, staring at my phone. I wondered if I should call instead of texting. Somehow, that seemed too awkward. I didn't want to call. He wasn't answering his text.

I was getting cold, so I pulled my jacket on. And I stared at my phone. And stared at my phone.

I tried texting again.

Hey?

Still nothing. Damn, I was going to have to call. I pushed the phone icon. It rang. It went through to his voice mail. "Hey. It's a phone. You know what to do."

I felt like such an idiot, but I had to leave a message. "Hey, um, it's Lizzie. I'm so sorry, I got waylaid, and I'm just now making it to the student union. I really didn't mean to stand you up. Give me a call if there's any way I can still join you guys!"

I hung up before I realized I hadn't given my phone number. And I was halfway back to my dorm room before I realized that you don't need to give phone numbers when leaving messages, the phone has the phone number right there.

Feb 18

Nathan never texted or called me back yesterday. This morning, I raced to Starbucks before my first class. He wasn't there. Michelle was, though.

"Michelle, is Nathan working today?"

"Not today. He'll be in tomorrow afternoon." She gave me a searching look. "Are you okay?"

"Yeah. No." I was ready to cry. "We were supposed to go to the thrift store together yesterday, but I got sidetracked and didn't make it. I texted him, and I called him, but he's not answering."

"Aw, I wouldn't worry about that too much. His phone is always dying. He missed his shift at work last week. If his sister didn't work here, too, I would never be able to get ahold of him."

I tried to feel better about the situation, but I wasn't completely convinced. It must have been written all over my face, because she gave me this sort of motherly pitying look, and then she handed me a caramel latte.

"Here you go, honey. Stop worrying. I can tell Nathan really likes you. He's not going to stop talking to you because you missed one date. Complications happen. It's not like you forgot you were supposed to meet him."

I was just taking a sip of my latte. I choked on it, and spluttered hot coffee onto my hands. Michelle handed me a paper towel.

"You need to calm down. Nathan's shift starts at 2:00. Come back tomorrow, and you can make everything right."

I nodded meekly. "Thank you for the latte."

She smiled and nodded, and then turned back to work as a couple of people walked up to the counter.

Feb 19

That was the longest 24 hours of my entire life. I didn't think 2:00 would ever come!

Finally! Spanish class got out at 2:30, I dumped my books into my bookbag, and literally ran all the way to the library. Well, I say that, but I ran until I was out of breath, then walked while breathing really hard, then ran some more. I got there as quickly as I possibly could.

Not my best plan ever, since it meant I showed up, flustered, out of breath, and no doubt all red and sweaty in the face. Yeah, that's attractive. Great way to impress a guy!

Both he and Natalie were working at the booth as I staggered up to it. Natalie saw me first. "Lizzie? What's wrong?"

"What's wrong is that I missed our outing," I gasped. I had a stitch in my side. "I'm so sorry. I was really looking forward to it, and then by the time I got over there, I was way too late to catch you guys."

Nathan smiled at me and handed me a caramel latte. I was really starting to enjoy this! "We figured you had a conflict. No biggie. We can try this again. It's not like we don't get to the thrift store something like every other paycheck." He looked keenly at me. "Did you run all the way here after your class?"

"You didn't answer my texts, so I figured you were mad at me," I answered.

He pulled his phone out of his pocket, and tapped at his screen. "Oh. You did text me a few times. Sorry. My battery was completely dead yesterday. Once I get it charged again, it forgets to tell me I had some texts while it was dead."

Michelle came over. "Hi, Lizzie. See, I told you there was nothing to worry about."

I shrugged a little self-consciously. "Yeah. Thanks."

She smiled at me. "So, this is a random question, but you don't happen to be looking for a job, are you?"

"Well, not really," I answered. "I've got a job over at the law library. Why?"

"I'm looking for another person to work here. I had a lot of people graduate last semester, and I still haven't replaced them all."

"I'll ask around," I promised.

"I'd appreciate that, thank you," she answered. There was a noise, and the quiet library was suddenly bursting with people. All the people I had outrun getting out of class were now here to get their coffees. "Speaking of shorthanded, time to get to work, you two."

Nathan and Natalie both smiled at me over the counter. "We were thinking of going to the Salvation Army way out on the end of University Drive, you want to go tomorrow?"

"Yes!" I answered. "I would love a second chance."

The line was getting seriously long. "I'll text you, I swear," Nathan told me, then he got back to work.

Feb 20

The trip to Salvation Army today was perfect. It turned out all three of us were done for the day at 3:30. We had a fun time riding over in his sister's car, which turned out to be an old white Cutlass Sierra. The bumper droops down a little at the front corner, and one of the windows doesn't roll up properly, and Natalie says the car likes to stall sometimes when waiting for a red light. But they are still wheels!

We sang to the radio together, and talked a lot. They told me about people-watching at the coffee shop, I told them stories about working at the circulation desk. We wandered around the thrift store, found a ton of things, tried them all on, kept some, rejected others, ventured opinions on each other's finds, and talked each other into or out of purchases.

We each came home with a big bag, and spent less than $10. We talked all the way home about our favorite thrift store finds. Natalie got the prize for best find; she once got a sweater for nine cents.

"It wasn't even that great of a sweater, but for nine cents, I had to buy it!" she said with this little competitive smirk. Damn, she is gorgeous. I never look at her without marveling how gorgeous she is. I'm so glad Nathan's her brother. I'd never, ever be able to compete.

"Of course, it was a moral obligation at that point," I agreed with her.

"See? I knew you'd understand," she said.

"It's still kind of an ugly sweater," Nathan chimed in.

"It's not THAT bad," Natalie protested.

"Are you kidding? It's so…. purple and pink," Nathan responded.

"So it's girly. I'm not asking you to wear it," Natalie answered.

Nathan was sitting in the back seat, he leaned forward to talk to me. "Our mother put us in matching outfits when we were kids. She liked to sew, which meant we'd have matching sweater vests or something, and Natalie'd have a skirt and I'd have pants for the same outfit."

I couldn't help but giggle at that thought. "Sounds adorable."

"Mom flipped out the day we switched bottoms. We were in sixth grade, and getting a little old for the twinsie thing. Natalie had this pleated skirt, so we switched and told everyone I was wearing a kilt. Everyone in school thought it was cool. Mom wasn't amused."

"That's hysterical! And very clever," I admired their creativity. "It must be fun having a built-in co-conspirator."

"It can be. It also means there's a built-in rival at all times," Natalie pointed out. "But we're good at pooling resources, instead of competing for them."

"That's so cool."

"Not to mention much smarter, if we do say so ourselves," Nathan agreed, with a cute kind of superiority.

Once Natalie parked the car, we wandered back toward the dorms with our loot. The twins' dorms are on a different part of campus than mine, so we sort of lingered in Fountain Square, which is about halfway in between, and talked.

Already I can't even say what it was we talked about. Telling stories about the worst birthday present we'd ever gotten. And the most memorable birthday we could think of. We all read web comics when we should be studying. None of us are into guns, and we have friends that are.

"I don't mean to break up the party, but would you two excuse me? I'm supposed to be meeting Laurel for dinner."

"You lost another bet with her, didn't you?" Nathan asked.

Natalie smiled sheepishly. "Yeah, kind of."

"Kind of? It seems to me bets are an either-or situation. You either won, or you lost," Nathan teased her.

Natalie mock glared at her brother. "Okay, so I lost another bet. Happy now?"

"Only when you tell me what stupid thing you bet on this time."

"I bet her that her break up with Jonathan wasn't going to last more than two weeks. I thought for sure he'd come crawling back to her. She said his pride was hurt, and there was no way he'd come back."

"And it's been three weeks now, I take it?"

"Worse than that, they were broken up two weeks and two days when he asked Leesa out."

"Laurel's best friend?" Nathan looked aghast.

"Yep." Natalie looked sullen. "So, what can I say. I owe Laurel dinner at that little Vietnamese place with the bowls of noodle soup bigger than your head."

"Mmmm, I love pho," I interjected. Partially to show off that I was sophisticated enough to know what it was called. And partially because they were gossiping about people I didn't know. I didn't mind really, and I felt bad for this Laurel person. "I'm going to have to remember that you like to lose bets with food at stake."

"Yeah, well, speaking of bets and debts, I need to go pay mine. See you guys later. This was really fun."

"Bye," Nathan and I said in unison. Then we laughed. After Natalie left, we found out that we both like every kind of Asian food we've ever tried; Chinese, Thai, Sushi, Korean, Vietnamese.

"You know what I want? I want a restaurant that has a buffet with every kind of egg roll on it. I would totally have an entire meal of nothing but egg rolls," Nathan fantasized.

"I love this idea, I would totally eat there," I agreed. "It needs to be one of those big buffet places. There could be a whole table devoted to soups, and one table of nothing but rice and rice noodles, and udon, and stuff."

"Mmm, and then a table devoted to dumplings. Every country has its own version of gyoza, don't they?" he asked.

"I think so. Let's see, then we'd need a table of meats. Someplace to put the General Tso's chicken and the bulgogi and the sweet and sour pork."

He smiled at me. "Is that where the sushi goes, too?"

I thought about it for a second. "I suppose that's where it goes. Fish is a meat, after all."

"Do we have to have a table for desserts?" he asked.

That gave me pause. "Asian sweets aren't very satisfying. Hard to compare fortune cookies to French pastries, or Italian gelato."

"But if we want this to be a truly cultural experience, we really ought to have those balls filled with red bean paste, and green tea ice cream."

I started laughing. "And we'd go out of business in a hurry if we didn't have fortune cookies."

He laughed with me. "Yes, yes we would." I like the way his eyes crinkle up at the corners when he laughs. "There is one very important thing we've still forgotten," he added.

"What's that?" I asked.

"Where do we put the crab rangoons?"

I had to think about that for a moment. "You know, I think we would have to give the crab rangoons their own separate little table. Maybe we can put them on a pedestal of their own."

He nodded. "Yes, yes, that would be appropriate."

We looked at each other, and inexplicably started laughing again.

"So if we're going to open up a restaurant together, I'll have to change my major," he said.

"What is your major?" Somehow, that hadn't come up in conversation yet.

"Computer science. What's yours?"

"I don't have a major right now. I've tried on a couple different majors, but I didn't find a good fit. I decided to get out quickly, before I committed to a lifetime doing a career I hate."

"So do we need to go for business management, or culinary arts?" he asked playfully.

"Maybe we need to double major in both?" I asked my own question. In the back of my mind I was thinking about Ken and his MBA vs. marine biology problem. This was a contrast, here's a guy cheerfully talking about changing his major, instead of whining about it. "Or we split up. One of us takes one major, the other of us takes the other major."

"Or we both go for entrepreneurship, because we're going to have to hire an awful lot of chefs. We'll need to have a Chinese chef, a Japanese chef, a Korean chef, a Vietnamese chef, and a Thai chef," he pointed out.

"We're going to need a really, really big kitchen," I agreed. We both started laughing again.

We must've stayed there talking for another two hours. When I finally walked home, I gave big happy grins to everyone I passed. I wanted to cavort around and hang off of lampposts, singing some sappy happy song about falling in love. There must be some such song in every musical ever made, right? I was a little afraid of looking too silly, but I did do a skippy little dance along the top of the retaining wall in front of the computer science building.

Feb 21

The "high" I was on last night hasn't worn off yet. I was so excited and happy I hardly slept last night, but I didn't even feel tired when I gave up and got up. I sang in the shower, and after I got dressed I figured I'd go to the library to study….and get coffee. I closed our dorm room door and took off doing pirouettes down the empty hall.

At least, I thought it was empty. Until I crashed into Lon, coming out of the door of the common room just as I was twirling past.

"Whoa, there, Margot Fonteyn." He had me by the shoulders, steadying me back onto my feet after I had plowed right into him. "The orchestra is thataway."

"Who's Margot… what's her name?" I asked. Talk about a contrast. Last night I'd been feeling so clever in my conversation with Nathan, and now Lon was making me feel like an ignorant country bumpkin.

"Margot Fonteyn. Famous ballerina. She used to partner Rudolf Nureyev."

"Wow, that's cool." At first I was sure I'd never heard of him either, but then I remembered. I think he was on the Muppet Show as a guest star, once. So he must have been really famous.

"At their first performance together in *Giselle*, they had 23 curtain calls."

I smiled and nodded. I had no idea what to say to that. Why does this computer nerd know anything about ballet? That seemed weird. But I wasn't going to ask. "That must have been amazing."

"I have trouble wrapping my brain around the concept of that many curtain calls," he said. "So what has you practicing your chainé turns down the hall this morning?"

"I'm in a really good mood today," I told him. "Last night I spent hours talking with one of the guys who works at the Starbucks in the library. That was so much fun." It's odd, I felt a little funny telling him about Nathan. Maybe because it's too early in the relationship to talk to anybody about it.

Lon's reaction was kind of odd. I think he sort of stiffened up. "I see. Well, enjoy the rest of your twirling. But keep an eye out for passers-by next time." He took his hands off my shoulders, nodded at me as if dismissing me, and marched off down the hall towards his room.

"Thanks, I will," I called after him. "And maybe later you can tell me more about this ballerina."

He stopped, and turned around to look at me. "I could, but somehow I doubt you have much interest in ballet."

"I'm interested in lots of things," I answered. The way he said it made me feel a little defensive.

"I'm sure you are, but I don't think you and I are generally interested in the same things," Lon said. He seemed to hesitate, then walked back over to me. "You know, I'm very glad that you turned me down when I asked you out at the beginning of our freshman year. You saved the both of us from wasting our time. You can claim credit for having more wisdom than me. It wouldn't have worked out. You're very pretty, but you're not my type."

"What's your type?" The question was out of my mouth before I could stop it.

"Honestly? Straight A students."

I didn't have a thing I could say to that.

"I'm not saying it to be mean, or anything," he went on. "I'm sure you're perfectly smart in your own way. They don't let people into college if they can't prove some level of sense and understanding. But since you asked, I'm answering. I like talking to girls about mathematical principles and have them talk back. Or cultural touchstones. Or social logistics. You and I wouldn't have that much in common to talk about."

I looked at him, dumbfounded. And here I'd been pretty sure that he still sort of had a thing for me. I've run into him in the hall or lobby so many times, I was starting to think he was lurking around, waiting to see me.

I couldn't think of anything to say - which kind of proves his point, doesn't it? "Yeah, maybe you're right. Of course, since we didn't try, we'll never know, will we?"

"I guess not," he answered stiffly. "Well, if you'll excuse me, I just pulled an all-nighter, I need to get a shower before I go to class."

I stood there a moment, watching him leave. I could have sworn his demeanor changed after I told him about my day with Nathan.

Mar 6

Boys are just plain confusing.

I walked into Spanish class today, and there was Ken!

He grinned at me when I walked in. "Hola, stranger!"

"Hola!" I tried to look glad to see him. "What are you doing here?"

"I transferred sections. How did you expect me to get through Spanish without my practice buddy? It's more fun being in class with you. I didn't have class during this time, so I switched."

Why, oh why did he have to be spoken for? The gesture was so sweet and… dare I say it? Romantic. What guy changes his class schedule for a girl? Talk about giving me mixed messages.

So, once again, I'm the 'buddy.' Just like with Eddie. Oh, goody. Well, a girl needs friends, right? I should just enjoy the fact that I have some smart, cute guy friends. Maybe they'll eventually hook me up with some smart cute friend of theirs.

I smiled at Ken and tried to put a good face on it. "That's great! I've been missing you, too." As soon as I said it, I had to wonder if that's a lie or the truth. I'm not sure.

"To be honest, my grades have been suffering without you to coach me. It's only six weeks into the semester, and I'm already worrying about my grade," he grinned at me. "I'm here so that you can whip me back into shape."

The words were out of my mouth before I could stop them. "I didn't know you were into whips."

He gave me this look back that couldn't get much more flirtatious. "I'm into all kinds of things."

"Including girls that are good at Spanish?" If he's going to flirt, I'm going to flirt back. Guys can be really bad at talking about things. Maybe he and Karla broke up, and that's why he moved to my section! It's not exactly the kind of thing you just blurt out. Although in my imagination I could very happily see him looking me in the eyes and saying "Karla and I broke up, and I thought you were really hot since we first started taking class together. That's why I warned you off that Darcy guy. I could tell you weren't into me then, but I was hoping that maybe now that we're both free, we can get together and see if we can make something happen?"

Sadly, that's not what he said. "Well, yeah. Karla suggested that I should call you and see if you'd get together to study with me, until I noticed that there was still time to change classes. I had to drop my section and register for yours, but the professor said it was okay. So, here I am!"

My heart sank. Sure didn't sound like he'd broken up with Karla. I might as well bite the bullet and find out where things really stand. "So how's Karla doing?"

I spent the next three minutes wishing I hadn't asked while he gushed about how wonderful Karla is, how smart she is, how funny she is, how she's always got the greatest advice, about how they're doing this new workout routine together. He even bragged about how good her cooking is. I've never been so happy for class to begin.

This is getting to be awful. I can't go near the math building without this nagging fear that I'll run into Professor Jacobson. I can't be around the dorm without being a little afraid I'll run into Lon. I can't call my best friend when I go home, because it's awkward with him, after his comment about my being disgusting. Now I won't be able to go to Spanish class without feeling like a moron. I desperately hope things work out with Nathan. Otherwise I have to give up drinking coffee.

Mar 27

I found bigger things to be mystified by than Lon's and Ken's behavior. This morning, Nathan's boss Michelle was acting even stranger.

I knew Nathan was working at 8, so I thought I'd stop in on the way to class. It was almost 9:30 when I got to Starbucks. "Hi, Michelle!" I called when I saw her.

She jumped, and spun around. She looked like a caged animal or contestant who is in the middle of losing at a game show. When she saw it was me, she sort of relaxed. "Oh, it's you." There was something fake about the smile she gave me.

"I thought I'd say a quick hi to you guys before I get to class," I told her. "I'm sorry, I didn't mean to startle you."

"You didn't startle me, I'm just waiting for Nathan to get back. I had to send him on an errand. We're almost completely out of every sort of dairy. No milk, no skim milk. All I've got is whipped cream."

If Nathan would have been the one telling me this, oh, the dirty jokes I would have made! "Wow, that doesn't get your day off to a good start," I sympathized. "Well, I should get to class. I hope your day gets better."

I turned to leave, but she called me back. "I can sort of fake your caramel latte for you, with the whipped cream," she offered.

"Nah, I appreciate all the free drinks, but I don't want to get you in trouble," I told her. "Especially when all you've got is your whipped cream until Nathan gets back with supplies."

"It doesn't matter. I'm already in plenty of trouble," she answered cryptically. I think she was joking – and I think she wasn't joking, at all.

I tried back later between classes, but the people working there were all people I didn't know. Which is a little odd... I

didn't know when Nathan got off, but I figured Natalie or Michelle would have been there.

I walked up to the counter to ask where they were, but I got stopped in my tracks by the conversation going on between one of the people behind the counter and someone on the other side of it.

"No, we haven't had any other complaints about food poisoning or anything," the gal behind the counter was saying. She was short, and round, and blonde with blue and purple streaks in her hair.

The other person was a tallish, skinny guy in a polo shirt and slacks. There was something about the way he was dressed that screamed "this is a uniform."

"Well, the person who filed the complaint with the Board of Health said that he suspects the person in charge of this facility." He was looking at his clipboard while he talked. "Were you working here on February 16?"

"Maybe," Blue-and-Purple Girl answered. "That's kind of a long time ago. You honestly expect me to remember which days I worked that long ago? I can't tell you what I did last weekend without some serious thought."

Mr. Clipboard gave her a look. Like the kind cops give in TV shows when they're questioning suspects in a murder investigation. "I assume you keep a calendar on your phone? Can you tell us if you were working two weeks ago Thursday?

Blue-and-Purple Girl pulled her phone out of her back pocket, and started tapping at the screen. "Yeah, after I got out of class, I worked til close," Blue-and-Purple Girl answered.

"And things looked pretty much the same then as they do now?"

She gave him another 'oh, get real' look. "Probably. It always looks the same around here. I don't remember ever coming in to work and saying gee, something looks different around here. Until today. Getting a visit from you today is definitely something different."

The health inspector – I assume that's what he was – was scribbling on the pages on his clipboard. When he finished he looked back up at her. "Do you remember your boss ever acting a little out of the ordinary?"

"No." She paused. "Well, there was one day when she was a little distracted. Some ex-boyfriend of hers had been annoying her."

"Would you be able to identify this ex-boyfriend from a photograph?" the inspector asked. Now I was wondering if he wasn't a health inspector, but maybe an undercover cop or something.

"No, I wasn't here when he came to see her. I just heard later that he had been here, and she was a wreck the rest of the day. So are you going to tell me what's going on?"

"A customer ended up in the hospital. He has been released, and he has filed charges blaming this Starbucks for poisoning him."

Blue-and-Purple gave him the most priceless look. "Poisoned him with what, dirty countertops? I doubt that. It's not like we keep arsenic next to the sugar. There's nothing here that's poisonous. This accusation is preposterous."

The inspector shrugged. "It's my job to do the inspections and ask questions."

"Well, what you see is pretty much what you get," she gestured around the little coffee shop. "We serve coffee. And a small selection of slightly stale baked goods. If we're guilty of anything, we're guilty of sabotaging your diet with way, way too much sugar. There are people who think sugar is poison, but they don't usually end up in the hospital."

I stopped listening, leaned against the back side of the shop, and gasped for air. Michelle had poisoned her ex-boyfriend!

Maybe Blue-and-Purple Girl didn't know what was going on, but I did. I'd seen it all happening. The pieces of the puzzle were all right there. The guy in the suit that she'd been arguing with. She told him to drop dead. Then he demanded coffee. She'd sloshed a drink together for him – AFTER SHE MOVED SOME CLEANING STUFF. That would be plenty poisonous to kill someone. Then she had come to talk to us, because we'd all been watching. Is that when she'd started giving me all the free caramel lattes?

Oh my god. She tried to murder her ex-boyfriend. And she was being nice to me because I was one of the witnesses.

And the other two witnesses were – Nathan and Natalie!

I had to talk to them. Both of them. Right away. Before she poisoned all three of us. I wondered if there was arsenic in the drinks she'd been giving me. Maybe Blue-and-Purple was wrong, and there really was arsenic next to the sugar. Obviously, if she was trying to kill me, she wouldn't do it right away. If she was clever, she'd put in a little bit every time. Can I go to the Student Health Center and get tested for arsenic?

I pulled my phone out, but my hands were shaking so badly, I dropped it on the ground. I dropped it again when I tried to pick it up.

A hand reached down and picked it up for me. It was the health inspector. Or undercover investigator, or whatever.

"You seem to have a case of the dropsies, today. Be careful, these phone cases are good, but they can only take so much," he warned me.

"You're right. Thank you," I mumbled, taking my phone from him.

I stared at him while he walked away. Should I chase him down, tell him what I know? What if Michelle found out that I told him, and hurried up and finished poisoning me for outing her, before they could arrest her? And what about Nathan and Natalie? I didn't want to endanger them. What was I supposed to do?

Finally I remembered the phone in my hand. I started texting Nathan and Natalie.

> Hey guys, can you meet me in the Square ASAP? Got news.

I sent it, then waited. And waited. And waited. Oh, my god, maybe they were already dead. Maybe Michelle finished them off, and their bodies are in the trunk of her car right now.

My heart started beating even faster than it already was. And I'd just texted them - so now she was going to come after me. At least I didn't say in my text anything about her. But if she was a crazy killer, it probably wouldn't matter. I was the third witness. I was probably still in just as much danger as they were.

I had to get away from there. She could be back any time now, and I didn't want her to see me. On the other hand, it was in the middle of the library. It doesn't get much more public than that. You can see the place in 3-D, from the first floor, of course, and from the balcony on the second level. So unless there's some sort of hidden basement right under the shop, there's no way not to be seen by lots of people, at all times. Except when the library's closed.

I was supposed to be on my way to Spanish class, but I had more pressing matters. I had to go to the Square, in case Nathan or Natalie got my message, but didn't text back. Of course, if they weren't texting back, that wasn't a good sign.

I had been pacing the Square a good ten minutes when I remembered the whole thing about Nathan's phone dying a lot. But then I remembered that it was Michelle who had told me not to worry if Nathan didn't text me back, his phone died a lot. Maybe she was setting me up even then. She was planning his demise even then, and telling me about the phone thing was designed to stop me from calling the cops the moment I realized he was missing. That would give her a few more hours to dispose of the body.

I was pacing faster now. A cyclist almost ran into me when I turned around to go back the way I had come. I wished I knew Nathan or Natalie's class schedule. I realized that, other than the fact that he's a comp sci major, and I know which dorm he lives in, I don't know much more about him. Other than the fact that he makes great caramel lattes and he likes thrift stores.

I thought about checking his dorm room. I didn't know which wing he was in, but I could go read all the mailboxes, right? That seemed like a good idea, until I realized I don't even know his last name.

All my brain was capable of by then was repeating oh my god oh my god oh my god, and regretting my choice not to talk to the health inspector. I wondered how one gets in contact with a health inspector.

My phone chirped at me. I'd been clutching it in my hands ever since I'd dropped it. I looked at the screen. It was Ken, asking why I wasn't in Spanish class. I ignored him. I put the phone in my pocket. If I kept clutching it like this, I would crack the screen or something, from the pressure of squeezing it.

I hadn't taken more than a few paces when my phone chirped again, and I was fumbling in my pocket to pull it back out. I almost dropped it again, but managed to catch it after bouncing it off my fingers a couple of times.

It was Nathan!

I'm on my way.

I stopped pacing the entire length of the Square, and stood where the two of us had talked for so long that night, planning our eggroll restaurant. I didn't know which direction he'd be coming from, so I walked in a little circle, trying to see 360 degrees at once.

Classes were obviously out, there were so many people! I wanted them all to go away. It had been relatively deserted the other night. I wish I would have thought to notice that night whether there were any stars out, or whether the moon had been out. The Square is pretty well lit, but we should have been able to see something. I guess all I could see was Nathan.

He was almost in front of me before I saw him. Obeying my first impulse, I ran and threw myself into his arms. "You're alive."

"Well, sort of, it was kind of a dull class," he laughed at my melodramatic greeting. "So what's your news?"

"It's about your manager at Starbucks. I was just there, the health inspector is investigating her. She tried to poison that ex-boyfriend of hers! You know, the one she was arguing with several weeks ago."

Nathan looked at me a moment. "What?"

"I went to go find you at Starbucks, and you weren't there, but a health inspector was. One of your customers ended up in the hospital, and reported your store to the Health Department. He's saying he was poisoned. And, Nathan," I pointed out, "remember how your boss had been fighting with that guy, and she'd told him to drop dead?"

Nathan was staring at me. "That's only a figure of speech."

"Are you sure it was in this case? Remember how she made his coffee afterwards, and…"

"Michelle did not poison anyone – her ex-boyfriend or anyone else," he interrupted me. "She's a sweet, generous person. She's fiesty, and she's the sort who will tell people to fuck off or drop dead. But she's not going to go killing anyone."

"But," I protested. I had to tell him the rest of my evidence.

"You're unbelievable. She gives you free lattes because she knows I like you, and you go accusing her of attempted murder!"

"Maybe they're more like hush money, to shut me up and keep me from talking. Or maybe there's poison in them. That's why I wanted to see you right away. You, me, and Natalie are the only witnesses. What if we're all being slowly poisoned?"

Nathan stared at me incredulously while I talked. The look he gave me was the most awful thing I've ever endured in my life. "I don't know you." He turned and started walking away from me.

"Nathan!" I was having trouble seeing him, my eyes weren't working right. "Please be careful. What if I'm right?"

He didn't turn around, but started walking even faster. "Nathan!" I sobbed.

I didn't run after him. What would I say when I got to him? What was I supposed to do, throw myself at his feet and throw my arms around his legs to keep him from leaving? Obviously, the thought occurred to me, but I wasn't so sure where it would go from there. From the look he gave me, I guessed he'd pull his legs out of my grasp and keep walking.

I don't know what scares me more: the thought that I might be right, and Nathan and Natalie (and I) might be in danger, or the thought that I might be wrong, and Michelle is innocent, and I have just screwed up my budding romance with Nathan for nothing.

Mar 28

Oh, goody, another night where I can't sleep. Might as well get my work done. If I can focus. Maybe Lon will be up working again, too. After telling me that we would have nothing in common, I kind of want to prove him wrong. At least I want to prove to him we can be friends, if nothing else.

I'm way behind in accounting class, anyway. I grabbed a pencil, my ledger, and my textbook, and turned on the light at my desk. Once again, I was sort of glad my roommate is never here, so I wasn't disturbing her.

On the other hand, being by myself all the time is too lonely. I made slow progress on my backlog of assignments, but the silence of my room was closing in on me.

I tried the upstairs common room, and the downstairs one. Lon wasn't in any of his usual spots. I wandered past his room. No lights coming from under the door. Not that I knew whether the doors to our rooms would leak any light. Probably not. I thought about going outside to see if there were any lights in the windows, but I figured that would be too creepy and stalker-like. I gave up, and found myself a comfy chair in the upper common room, where I see Lon working most of the time.

It's stupid trying to concentrate on a page when all you can think about is other things, so I might as well write in here for a while. There is, at least, one teensy, small ray of hope in the midst of all this. Nathan said he liked me. Michelle was giving me free coffee because he liked me.

Now, whether or not that's true, is one thing. Maybe she was, and maybe she was trying to poison me because I was a witness. Just because Nathan doesn't believe it, doesn't mean I'm wrong. He wasn't there to hear the investigator's questions.

Maybe once the investigator interviews him and Natalie, then he'll believe me.

That makes me feel better. Of course, the investigator will be talking to Nathan and Natalie, they were the ones working that day! Once he talks to them, then Nathan will understand why I'm so alarmed. Then he'll forgive me.

Oh my god - I might have inadvertently done the worst thing possible! What if Nathan tells Michelle what I said, before the investigator talks to Nathan and Natalie? If Michelle is tipped off, it will put Nathan in more danger, not less. Michelle might know that they're onto her, and then she knows she needs to eliminate her eyewitnesses.

I wish I knew exactly where Nathan's room is! I want to go sit outside his door like a security guard, just to make sure Michelle doesn't get to him before the police, or the health department, or whoever that guy was, talks to him.

Of course, even after that I guess there's a danger that Michelle can still poison him somehow, out of revenge instead of to hush him up.

What if I'm wrong about Michelle's character? What if the guy was poisoned by accident somehow? That seems pretty weird and unlikely. Of course, if he is a big asshole, he probably has other enemies besides his ex-girlfriend. Maybe someone else has done the deed, and Michelle's coffee is just circumstantial?

So, I guess the question comes down to whether or not I'm wrong about Michelle's character. If I'm right, I guess I'm exonerated. If I'm wrong, will Nathan forgive me? Henry Tilney forgave Catherine Morland for her suspicions about his father.

I give up, I'm putting away the ledger. I'm not getting any work done. I'll try working on my photography project instead. There's a view down the street from the window here that might give me some cool time-lapse exposures. It's worth a try. Even in the middle of the night like this, there are still cars passing by.

I wonder where Lon is. There's something reassuring about him. I wonder what he'd say if I told him about what was going on. He seems like such an engineer – he likes fixing problems. I wonder if he's broken up with Larissa. I haven't seen her since the night I went with her to the emergency room. Next time I see him, I'll ask him about her.

Mar 29

So I ended up falling asleep in the chair. I was so frantic about it when I woke up, I packed up the camera, ran back to my room, showered, dressed, and was in the elevator before I discovered it was only 7:30. So what the hell - since I was already out the door, I just went to the little flower stand in the student union and bought an iris as a peace offering.

I got to the library about ten minutes after they opened. I tried to look nonchalant as I approached Starbucks. I mean, after all, if Michelle was there, I didn't want to look like I knew her secret.

There was a strange guy there with Purple-and-Blue Girl, and Natalie. No Nathan, no Michelle. He was clearly giving instructions to the two girls. When I walked up to the counter, I could see he's wearing a badge that says "District Manager." That didn't bode well. He turned around when he realized I was standing at the counter. "What can I get you this morning?"

Wow, he was good. A second ago, he was frowning and growling at his employees. Now he was all charm with a big Irish smile. I guess that's why they pay him the big bucks. "I'd like a caramel latte, please," I said, trying to catch Natalie's eye.

"What size?"

"Venti, please." He took my money while Natalie was making my order. "Is Michelle working today?" I had to ask.

His face became very bland. "I'm sorry, Michelle no longer works here. Are you a friend of hers?"

I shook my head. "She just always seems to be here."

"Yes, well, she won't be any more." That was all he said. He seemed overly eager when another customer walked up to the counter. "Good morning, what can I get for you today?" I was clearly dismissed.

I was afraid to chit chat with Natalie with the big boss guy standing right there. I waited until she brought me my latte. "What happened to Michelle? And, is Nathan working today?"

"He'll be in around 11:00. Michelle got fired. Apparently she was dipping into the till," Natalie whispered to me.

"She was embezzling?" I whispered back. Natalie nodded. Then she said, maybe a trifle too loudly, "The napkins are over there on the side, next to the sugar."

"Thank you." I was probably also a little bit too loud.

Now I'm sitting here in the sweet spot with no friends around, sipping my coffee, and wondering how I'm going to manage to live for the next three hours. I don't have physical education until 9:30, so I have over an hour to take some more photos. If I skip hotel management right afterwards, or duck out halfway through, I can be back at the library when Nathan gets in. I have to see him with my own eyes. Maybe that's why Michelle embezzled: she murdered Nathan last night at close, stuffed his body in her trunk, grabbed all the money in the till, and she's been driving all night. I wonder how long a person would have to drive to get to Mexico or Canada from here. If she stole cash, the authorities won't be able to trace her movements, will they? We'll have to hope that the customs agents at the border pay attention to the notices with the faces of fleeing criminals.

I hope Nathan is alive! After all, I have a flower for him.

I was right about Michelle. I don't know for sure yet if she's a murderer, but I was right that she's a criminal.

At least with her gone, I know it's safe to drink my caramel latte.

That is, unless Natalie is some sort of accessory. For all I know, she's in cahoots with Michelle. Even more awful, maybe Nathan and Natalie and Michelle are all part of some sort of crime ring. And that's why Nathan got so mad when I told him my suspicions. I'm too close to the truth.

Maybe I don't want to see Nathan, after all.

No, I have to. I have to know that he's alive. I would rather that he's a criminal, and alive, than dead because Michelle poisoned him. Whether or not I want to date him if he's a criminal of some sort, I don't know. I'll think about that later.

Right now, I need to try to concentrate on getting some work done. I always have my camera with me this semester, there has to be some sort of shots that look really good in this early morning light.

Mar 30

After phys ed, I decided to at least go to the beginning of hotel management. I figured I might as well not skip a class totally, when attendance is part of your grade. Better to slip out partway through.

I sat right next to the door, and then at 11:10, I collected my stuff, carefully picked up my iris which had managed to survive getting dragged around all morning from place to place, and slipped out the door.

For the second time in one day I ran to the library. Or, run/walk/pant/run some more. I must really like this guy.

Nathan was behind the counter when I got there. I could see him from the top of the stairs as I looked down into the library. I stood there a moment, staring at him, gripping the stair rail for support, and all I could think was "Oh, thank goodness. He's alive. He's okay."

Finally I pried my fingers off the railing and walked down the stairs, never taking my eyes off the coffee shop. I could see that the district manager guy was still there. There was also a brunette girl who I think was working when the health inspector guy was there.

I wasn't quite sure how to approach. Would the district manager not like it if his employees said hello to their friends? That seemed kind of likely. I didn't want to get Nathan in trouble. I looked down at my iris. Why did I buy it for him? To say I'm sorry? I guess that was it. I wasn't sorry that I'd been so alarmed, especially when it turned out I wasn't completely wrong about Michelle. But I was sorry I'd upset Nathan. And now he was learning that Michelle wasn't completely aboveboard, so I was sorry that he was probably having a lousy day today.

I decided maybe the best thing to do was to kiss up to the boss. I lurked around, watching, until the after-class rush died down. It was the longest 10 minutes of my life. Except for all the multiples of 10 minutes that had occurred since I started wondering if Nathan was alive.

I made sure my coat was open so my cleavage was showing, and I fluffed my hair a little. I thought about freshening my lip gloss, but I thought that might be a bit much. So I licked my lips to make sure they were shiny. Then I walked up to the counter.

"Hi, remember me?" I asked the manager.

He gave me a quizzical look along with his gorgeous Irish smile. "I'm sorry, should I?"

"I stopped in several hours ago. I've got a policy question for you."

Now I had his attention. "A policy question?"

"I wanted to find out if an employee would get in trouble if his girlfriend stopped in," I raised my flower and showed it to him, "long enough to say hello." Okay, that was pretty cheeky of me to claim that I was his girlfriend, but maybe it would make it more okay from a manager's point of view. I wasn't saying that I wanted to tie up his employee's time trying to flirt with him.

He looked at my flower, then he looked over at Nathan. "Oh, I see. Yes, you can say a quick hello. Although I'm not sure if he's allowed to keep that back here. I guess he can put it with his coat."

I smiled at him. "Thank you. I promise, I won't be but a minute."

I walked down to the end of the counter where the barristas hand over the finished beverages. Nathan was cleaning. I realized after a moment he deliberately wasn't looking at me.

"Hey," I said softly.

"I am not your boyfriend," he answered. He sounded sullen. I suppose he could be mad at me for being right about Michelle being a criminal. Or maybe he was mad that I'd called myself his girlfriend. He hadn't exactly asked me. It was a little early in the relationship to be using those terms.

"I know," I answered. "I thought if I said that, your manager would cut you some slack. I didn't know how much trouble you'd be in if I talked to you. Or if I gave you this." I held out the iris to him.

"I'm not taking your flower," he answered. He still wasn't looking at me. He was going to polish the coffee machines until I went away, or until he wore the finish off of them. I could tell that much.

"I wanted to say I'm sorry I made you angry. And considering what you guys have learned about Michelle…"

His face was starting to turn red. Then he looked at me, and I wished he hadn't. His expression was awful. Full of hatred for me.

"You don't know anything about Michelle," he told me.

"But," I started to protest.

"I think you'd better leave now." He was back to not looking at me again.

"But at least let me…"

"You promised my boss you were only going to be here a minute," he pointed out coldly. "I think you should keep your promise."

I went to lay the iris on the counter.

"Don't do that," he snapped. "You think the health department approves of us having foliage lying around on the countertops? Take it with you."

"I…" I couldn't think of anything to say at that point. All I could do was walk away.

I went over to the library's circulation desk. The lady behind the counter was probably old enough to be my mother. "Hi, this is going to sound like an odd sort of question, but are you having a good day or a bad day today?"

She gave me a curious look. "Well, I guess my day hasn't been particularly good, or particularly bad. That is an odd sort of question. Why do you ask?"

I handed her the iris. "Well, I hope the rest of your day goes a little bit better, then."

She took the flower from me. "Well, thank you. I guess it will, at that."

The pleasantly surprised look on her face did make me smile a little as I walked away. I like that adage about practicing random acts of beauty, or however exactly that goes. I should look it up, since I don't remember it word for word. I've seen it on bumper stickers before.

Apr 4

The last several days have been awful. I've tried texting him. He doesn't text back. I've stopped in at the coffee shop. I can't seem to catch either him or Natalie at work. I've discovered I don't have Natalie's phone number, so I can't text her to find out what's going on. Maybe she'd be willing to talk to me, even if Nathan isn't.

Once again, this isn't going according to the script. In *Northanger Abbey*, Henry Tilney forgives Catherine for suspecting his father of murder. I suppose maybe I'm being impatient. How much time elapsed before Henry came to propose to Catherine? More than a few days. So maybe I am going to have to suffer with doubt and self-recrimination for a few weeks, until my Henry – that is Nathan – comes around. Catherine had no communications with Henry until he came to see her and explained everything.

Apr 6

I had prepared myself for weeks of silence, but here it's only been two days and Nathan answered my texts.

Michelle did NOT take money from the till. Her boss, the regional manager, had been skimming things off. She was trying to cover his tracks, because they were dating. When he got caught, he turned around

and blamed her. Next time
you try to make friends,
don't go jumping to
conclusions.

That was it. I tried apologizing. I tried asking more questions. I tried calling him instead of texting. I tried going to Starbucks. There's a new manager there; I asked for Nathan's work schedule. Turns out, neither Nathan nor Natalie works there anymore.

I was beyond desperate. At least I know where the comp sci building is, and which dorm he lives in. I took to hanging out near the entrances or in the lobbies, hoping I would catch him coming by. Not a good way to get one's homework done.

Finally my vigilance paid off. I was working on my Spanish homework on a bench outside the front doors of his dorm, and he was walking toward the building. I jumped up, leaving my books on the bench, and ran up to him, calling his name.

He stopped and looked at me. "What are you doing here?"

"Trying to talk to you." I would think that part would be a little obvious.

"We have nothing to talk about." He started walking again.

"We have a lot to talk about!" I protested. "Look, I'm sorry I misjudged your boss. But obviously, so did a lot of other people. Can you blame me for taking things at face value?"

He stopped walking. Well, that was an improvement. "Yeah, I guess I do blame you for taking things at face value. She was really nice to you, but the moment you heard something bad about her, from a complete stranger, you passed judgment against her. That says something about you that I don't like."

"I was only thinking about you!" I protested desperately. "I was worried that I'm a bad judge of character, and that she wasn't as nice as she seemed, and you might be in danger."

Nathan looked up at the sky and shook his head. "Well, then, if you're that much of a drama queen, I don't think that reflects well on your character, either. Look, just go away. I have no interest in seeing you again."

It started raining as he walked away from me, and went into his dorm. I stood there, watching him go, feeling like an idiot, and very aware of how perfectly cinematic this all was. My life could be a movie. This would be where the camera would get a close shot of my face, so everyone could see that I was crying while the raindrops were also running down my face.

It started raining harder, and my hair was starting to get plastered to my head. This wasn't cinematic anymore, this was cold, wet, and uncomfortable. It was time to go home.

I have one of those little travel umbrellas somewhere in my dorm room. I really ought to put it in my book bag. It wouldn't have helped at this moment, since I'd left my stuff on the bench while I talked to Nathan. I threw the wet books into my wet bag.

I trudged home. I was glad that the Myth Busters proved that you don't get any less wet running through the rain than you do walking through it, because I didn't have the energy to run. I had done enough running on Nathan's behalf. I didn't need to do any more.

Because my head was down, I didn't even see Lon when I plowed right into him in front of our dorm. "Oh! Sorry," I mumbled. "I seem to have developed this bad habit of running into you. Literally."

He was all dry and dignified under a big, black golf umbrella. Even his book bag was dry. The only thing wet was the round spot on his chest where I'd run into him. Wow, I didn't know I was really that wet.

He had stepped in close to me, to hold the umbrella over the both of us. "You look like you're having a lousy day."

"Yeah. I guess you could say that's an understatement," I agreed. "I'm learning some life lessons that aren't much fun."

"Life lessons never are," he started walking us both toward the shelter of our dorm.

"I guess. I don't suppose this will come as a shock to anybody who knows me, but I don't think I'm much good at figuring people out."

"Do you mean you're abandoning a career in psychology, or you don't think you're a very good judge of character?" he asked me.

"Both. Or, is that neither? I'm apparently a lousy judge of character, and because of that, I'd better not try going into psychology. I would suck at it."

Lon had gotten us under the eaves by front of the door, and he shook the water off his big umbrella before he rolled it and used the little strap to snap it shut. I wondered while I watched him if there's a name for the little strap with the snap on the end that keeps umbrellas all nice and tidy when you close them. Even the umbrellas that come with a condom to keep them packed up still have the little strappy thing.

I stopped watching his hands on the umbrella and looked up into his face. Damn, he's tall. He was smiling down at me with this very kind expression. "No, I don't suppose you are very good at figuring people out. At least you're not alone. Lots of people aren't. If it were easy, everybody would be doing it."

I wasn't sure I knew what he meant by that. I opened my mouth, but decided against saying anything. Whatever I said was going to be stupid. I was tired of being stupid today.

"Now, you go get out of those dripping wet clothes and dry off. Maybe you can avoid getting sick if you get warm as quickly as you can. If you knock on my door, I've got a bottle of whiskey in my room. I can make you a hot toddy. My mother swears a hot toddy cures everything but AIDS."

"Is a hot toddy tea, and booze, and honey?" I asked.

He smiled that kindly smile again. "Pretty much."

"I've got all that in my room." Then I realized that was kind of rude of me, like I was blowing him off. Again. "But can I knock on your door if I have any questions?"

"Of course. You can always knock on my door if you have questions."

"Okay. Thanks."

A hot shower took the chill off my body, but nothing seems to be able to shake the chill I have in my brain. Over the last two years, I have lived through *Pride and Prejudice*, *Sense and Sensibility* - twice - *Mansfield Park*, and now *Northanger Abbey*. If one could say that Lon is Captain Wentworth, I've also been living *Persuasion* in slow motion since my first day of college. Never, never does real life come out to be anything like a Jane Austen story! I always thought that Jane wrote stories that are observations of life. My brother was right, I was wrong. She didn't write about life. She wrote fairy tales. Everyone is always telling me I'm delusional, why haven't I been listening?

I'm going with "I'm an optimist" for my answer, for now. But that's it, I've learned my lesson. No more Jane Austen. She lied to me. The twists and turns of the heart never end up with an admission of love.

This is what I get for relying upon a spinster as my model of what romance is like. What was I thinking? I wanted it to be true so badly, I couldn't see Jane's writing for what it is. The fantasies of a lonely woman who never married. I am angry with Jane, but I'm even more angry with myself for taking so long to figure things out.

May 22

Coupled with my search for the meaning of life, the plan to figure out what I'm going to be when I grow up seems to be something of a failure. I tried taking courses in all these different areas, to figure out what I like and what I'm good at. But all I can say now is that I suck at everything.

My grades for accounting and physical education were about as good as my grades for chemistry. The photography teacher gave me a C and said that I simply don't have the "eye" for photography. Whatever that means. I didn't do much of anything artsy and fancy for the portfolio I turned in for class, but let's face it. I bet most of the people making a living with photography are shooting clothes for catalogues, or school pictures of kids, and weddings. None of these require artistic photoshop techniques or goofy angles. Still, if the teacher says I'm no good at photography, what are the chances I'd be able to get a job as a photographer?

At least I got a B in both marketing and hotel management. But I must say, neither class excited me very much. At least I got an A in Spanish.

Now that I'm home for the summer, I called up my old boss and got my job at McDonald's back. My parents didn't like it, but, of all people, Wendy was the one who convinced them to leave me alone. I overheard her and Mom talking in the living room when I came home from work today.

"At least she's got a job. Would you rather she just sat around the house all day for three months, eating ice cream? Or she could have worked in the law library all summer instead of coming home to see us. So why don't you lay off her?"

"But we're worried about her. We want her to be happy," my mother told her.

"She's happy working at McDonald's." If it wasn't for the fact that I was eavesdropping, I would have gone up and given Wendy the biggest hug.

"There's no future in McDonald's. What kind of salary can she make? What kind of man will she meet, working there?"

"That's what you're really worried about, your future son-in-law?" Wendy was on a roll. "If she can't find a decent guy in college, maybe she's better off meeting a guy at McDonald's."

"Is she even trying to find a decent guy in college?" my mother asked.

Wendy made this funny sort of whooshing sound of disgust. "You really need to get on Facebook, mom. Then you'd know what's going on in her life. She probably spends more time thinking about guys than she does thinking about a career."

"That would explain the bad grades," my mom said sourly.

"Well, make up your mind, do you want her to have good grades, or do you want grandbabies someday?" I made up my mind that when I get my first paycheck from McDonald's, I'm going to get her something really, really nice. A concert ticket, maybe. Or we could go shoe shopping.

"Is it too much to ask to have both?" Mom was sounding even more sour.

"Geez, Mom, you don't live in the real world." I could hear that Wendy was getting up to leave the room, so I backed up to the door, and closed it loudly just in time for her to come around the corner.

"So, you want to go do something fun when I get my first paycheck?" I asked her. I figured I didn't have to explain why I was being nice to her.

"Can you afford to do anything fun?" She gave me a skeptical look. "You're going to be in college for fifty years before you figure out what you're gonna do with the rest of your life."

Okay, so maybe Wendy wasn't really defending me, she just likes being bitchy to everyone. I'll still do something really nice with her when I get my first paycheck, anyway.

JUNIOR YEAR

Aug 18

Overhearing Wendy's conversation with my mom got me thinking, and I've decided to swear off men altogether this year, as well as swearing off Jane. They're a distraction, a source of pain and aggravation, and I really don't want to be in college for fifty years.

I've also decided to go with my strengths. I always get As in Spanish. So I'm going to declare a Spanish major!

It never occurred to me that language could be a career option. It was my brother David who gave me a boot to the head. I told him that foreign languages will be handy when going on vacation, but what else are they good for?

He gave me the classic little brother look. "You mean, like working as a translator at the UN? Or becoming a diplomat for the government? Or working at some big company that does business with the entire continent of South America? Or you could be a high school Spanish teacher."

When he finally stopped talking, I stood there, staring at him, feeling like an idiot. He was right. I just got the best career advice I'd ever had from a 12 year old.

"Are you going to call me a moron, if I tell you you're right?" I finally said.

"I don't need to tell you you're a moron, you already know it," he said. Then he shrugged. "But if you really were a moron, you wouldn't admit that I'm right."

I spent another one of my paychecks on doing something really nice for him, too. It cost me a lot of money, but a day of roller coasters and too much sugar was fun. And it cost me about the same as the waterslide park that Wendy and I went to.

I'm going to love my Spanish major. Besides the continuation of the Spanish language classes I've been taking all along, I've got a class on Spanish literature, a class on Spanish cinema, and a class on Hispanic cultures. I'm also taking beginning webpage design. It just seems like the practical kind of thing that some employer would love to see on my resume someday.

Aug 24

This is going to be fun! I've got an apartment close to campus with Tiffany and Allie. I've known them both since our freshman year, we're all part of the library sweet spot crowd. I'm carrying in a box of kitchen essentials Allie's mom gave us (the problem with apartments instead of dorms is that now you have to move cooking equipment as well as bedding and clothing), and who should be holding the door open for me, but – Lon!

"Well, hello!" he said when he saw my face.

"Wow, hi," I said. Then neither one of us knew what else to say.

"I'll chat with you when your arms aren't quite so full," he gave me this sort of courteous little bow.

"That will be great," I answered. "See you around!"

I suppose if he was really being a gentleman he would have offered to carry my box for me. But then, he was probably in the process of moving himself in, too. I was standing in front of my door when I realized I should have asked him what apartment he's in.

That's when I remembered my vow. I've sworn off men this year. It doesn't matter if I regret saying no when he'd asked me out two years ago. He is NOT Captain Wentworth, I am NOT living in a Jane Austen novel, and I won't distract myself with men when I need to focus on school.

"Hey, stop standing there and open the door!" Allie appeared in the hallway with her arms full of bedding. Her mother and sister were right behind her, carrying laundry baskets with towels in three colors, so all three of us girls will have color coded towels.

"Sorry." I put down the box and fished around in my pocket for the keys.

Allie was watching me. "Is something wrong?"

"I should have used smaller boxes. This thing is heavy," I said. I decided I wasn't going to tell Allie or Tiffany about Lon. If I'm swearing off men, what good will come of gossiping about them?

Sept 12

Sad thing about avoiding men, I feel like there's not that much else to talk about. Class is class. Spanish cinema is really fun, I can actually comprehend most of the movies without reading the subtitles! It's nice to be able to cheat sometimes, but I usually get the gist of it. Spanish literature is harder, because when I don't understand a word, I have to look it up. In cinema, if you miss it, you miss it. The movie keeps on going. Fortunately, the nonverbal parts can help.

Ken isn't taking Spanish anymore. He declared his major in bio-medical engineering. Whatever that means. It does mean he doesn't need to take Spanish. He's taking lots of math and biology instead. It gives me kind of mixed feelings. I miss him, but I don't miss feeling flustered over him being my friend while being involved with Karla. Now that I don't see him much, I only have to face down my feelings occasionally, when he sends me some random message to say "hola." I thought about making a case for Spanish as prep for Doctors Without Borders, but – no men this year!

The rest of the men in my past are pretty well staying in the past. Darcy Fitzwilliam must have graduated law school by now, I never see him at the law library anymore. I do make a point of avoiding the math building, and Professor Jacobson. Surprisingly, I still haven't heard from Eddie. Which is fine with me. If I disgust him so much, well, screw that. I crossed paths with Nathan the other day: that was awkward. I smiled and said hi. He looked at me and grunted and nodded his head. That was it.

I keep finding myself watching for Lon when I'm coming and going from the apartment. Sad thing about apartments vs. dorms, there's fewer common spaces, so less opportunity to mingle with other residents. In that way, I like dorm life better. But then again, I've sworn off men. So this is a good thing. I can't go seeking out Lon all over the building. Although I did look at the mailboxes and found out his room number. In case I need help with the webpage design class. He's the nerdy type, I'm sure he knows how to do this stuff.

Sept 18

Michael Knox called me out of the blue! I was writing my paper for Spanish lit, and getting stuck on what to say next. Michael's call was a welcome interruption. He reminded me about our ice cream date last year, when he was bringing in building proposals. His estimates have been accepted, and his firm is going to be doing some big renovations on campus.

"I'm going to be on campus tomorrow, would you like to get together for dinner after my meeting? My treat."

"Can it be an off-campus experience?" I asked hopefully.

"Hm, there's a new Thai place I've been wanting to check out, but I know you don't like Thai food."

"Where did you get that idea? I love Thai food," I answered.

"Since when?"

"Since as long as I can remember," I snorted.

"Well then you can't remember very long, because I recall you not liking Thai food."

"Look, are we going out for dinner or not?" I challenged. "Because if you're offering, but you won't take me to a new Thai place, you can tell me where it is, so I can find some friends with a car and go there myself."

"Okay, okay, I'll take you out for Thai," he laughed. "I can swing by your place around 5:30, 6:00. I'm not exactly sure how late this meeting is going to go."

"Don't you get to decide things like that, when you're a big important guy with your own company?" I asked.

"No, when you own a company, you're at the mercy of your clients. Especially big clients with multiple projects. When they want to talk, I listen," he explained to me in impatient, condescending tones.

"Well, don't get offended if I don't know these things. I don't run my own design firm," I reminded him.

"You never will if you keep changing your major," he pointed out.

"Well, you're going to remain a bachelor all your life, if these are the best manners you can come up with when you're calling to invite a girl out to dinner."

"Inviting you out to dinner isn't the same as asking a girl on a date," he retorted.

"You could have had me fooled. See you around 5:30 or 6:00." I have long since figured out that if I change the subject and then abruptly end the conversation, it is almost like winning an argument with him. Almost.

At least when he came to pick me up he seemed to be in a better mood. "You look nice. You didn't have to dress up on my account."

"What makes you think I dressed up on your account?" But of course I had. If I get to leave campus, it's a special occasion! I wore a leather skirt, a killer silk blouse I'd gotten from my last thrift store quest, and the cutest shoes! Anne gave them to me. They're brown heels with buckles on the sides and brown plaid on the parts that aren't leather. They demand that you look at my legs when I wear them. The fact that they make me two and a half inches taller is a bonus.

"Well, you look nice, whatever the reason. Ready to go?"

"I was born ready."

"No you weren't. You were born two weeks late. Your mother was doing all sorts of things like eating lots of spicy food and taking really long walks to try to convince you it was time to come out."

"It's kind of weird that you know that."

"Your mother whined a lot about being pregnant. I was almost seventeen when you were born. I was understandably curious about mating rituals at the time, and since pregnancy is one of the consequences of sex, my folks made sure I spent a lot of time with your mother. And then with you while you were an infant. I changed a lot of your diapers."

I gave him a tired look. "That's why you're still single, you know. You're probably still a virgin because you got too much sex education because of me."

"Don't be ridiculous. You've met my girlfriends." He's particularly annoying when he's so complacent while we're sparring like this.

I smiled, because I knew I had the winning shot this time. "That's not proof you had sex with any of them. The fact that they're all ex-girlfriends might be proof that you didn't have sex with any of them."

He opened his mouth, then shut it again. Finally, he had to admit defeat. "That's not fair, young lady. About the only way I can prove to you that I've had sex with any of them would be to show you photos of us naked together, and that would be in highly questionable taste, if not illegal. A gentleman would never do that. Aren't you still a minor?"

"Naked photos wouldn't be conclusive proof of sex. They could be posed, after you drugged them, or you paid them," I pointed out. "So, you're just going to have to concede defeat. How did your meeting go?"

He wouldn't accept defeat. He would have found ways to argue around it. He should have been a lawyer, not an architect or whatever. But if he just answered my question, he could stop arguing with me. I was glad he chose that route.

"It went very well. I got the contract, and I am pretty happy with the budget they agreed to."

We both tried to remain civil for the rest of dinner. Mostly because I kept asking questions and made him talk about himself the whole time. He's usually in pretty good humor as long as he's talking about himself.

Oct 25

I have to admit, it's kind of fun having Michael Knox on campus a lot. Almost every other Wednesday he seems to be calling me up to say he's on campus, and he'll buy me dinner. Sometimes he's here every week, and one time he was here three times in one week.

Even an adventurous soul like me can only have so many off campus experiences, however. I have a lot of papers due, so I don't always have the time to do anything fancy. Instead of going someplace fun, now he's taking me to the usual local places. We've been eating lots and lots of pho at the place across the street from the library.

Today I invited Tiffany to join us. I feel like I keep seeing less and less of my roommates, we're all so caught up in our lives and classes. So when she walked in to our place right as I was leaving to meet Michael for dinner, I talked her into coming with me.

"As long as I'm not intruding," she hesitated. "Wouldn't it be weird, my coming along on your date?"

"He's not my date," I explained, "he's more like my big brother."

"Okay, then. If you're sure."

"I'm sure. I feel like I haven't seen you all week. Come on."

We walked down to the lobby where Michael was waiting. I made introductions, then we walked over to Chipotle. I was really in the mood for their spicy salsa tonight.

Michael politely asked Tiffany all the usual questions, what was her major, how was she enjoying her classes, did she have any papers due yet, what was she going to do over Christmas break.

"I really ought to get a job, like Lizzie, so I can have a little more cash on hand. I feel like I'm constantly wondering how I'm coming up with my part of the electric bill, or where I'm getting money for groceries. It's hard to job hunt when I've got projects due all the time, and tests to study for." Tiffany changed her major last year from biology to broadcasting, now she always seems to have a deadline looming. "I don't know when I'm supposed to have the time to go look for something."

By now we were seated at Chipotle with our various tacos and burritos. Michael very gallantly paid for Tiffany as well as for me. Poor college students appreciate the generosity of older adults with good jobs. "So you don't have a job right now?" he asked.

"No, my parents wanted me to focus on school, so they didn't make me get a job. But they're not helping me with expenses all that much, and the money my grandma had left me for college is almost completely gone now," Tiffany explained anxiously. "School costs a lot more than it did when she passed away."

I looked at Michael. "Hey, doesn't your design firm hire extra help sometimes?"

Michael gave me one of his looks. "Sometimes. Usually we only take interns over the summer."

"Paid internships?" I asked.

He gave me a withering look. "Not usually."

"By 'not usually' you mean 'no,' don't you? Why don't you just say no?" I asked.

"Because it's rude," he answered. He gave me a look that told me I was being rude bringing up the idea of him offering Tiffany a job right in front of her.

"Since when is networking rude?" I asked Michael. He might be a hypocrite and not willing to say what he's thinking, but I'm not.

"When I don't have anything to offer that will help your friend," he answered.

"That's okay," Tiffany shrugged at us. "I'm not offended. I appreciate you thinking about me. I'll figure something out."

I was already onto another idea. I looked at Michael. "Your dad might know of something." His dad worked at a big insurance company, and I bet they're always hiring new people. It must be pretty dull work, so they probably have people quitting all the time. But the money must be good, the place has this giant fancy campus with a lobby that has palm trees and waterfalls in a giant atrium.

"My father doesn't exactly do the hiring and firing there, I doubt he can be much help," Michael answered.

"Well, we can ask him if he knows of anything, can't we?" I asked.

"He won't," he told me.

I was annoyed enough by his defeatist attitude, I pulled out my phone. I have his dad's number on my phone. "What's the point of having smart phones if we don't use them?" I scrolled through my contacts list, and hit the button. "No time like the present."

The phone rang three times, and then his dad answered. "Hi, Pops! It's Lizzie. Um, I mean Beth."

"Beth! How are you, young lady? And to what do I owe the pleasure of this call in the middle of the week? Are you in jail and need to get bailed out?" he laughed.

"No, Pops, nothing like that. I'm having dinner with Michael and another friend of mine, and it came up that she's looking for a job. I don't suppose you are aware of any openings at your work that would be compatible with a college student's schedule?"

"I can certainly take a look. Is this really for a friend, or are you asking for yourself and you're trying to be coy about it?"

"No, it's really for a friend," I giggled. "The law library

isn't firing me anytime soon, I hope. Actually, they might let me earn some extra money over Christmas break. They ordered some new materials that will be coming in this December, and they'll need some extra help cataloging it."

"Isn't all that online by now? I would have thought libraries were a thing of the past."

I was impressed at how progressive he was. "Well, maybe, but I hope not until I get out of college. For now, it's still a resource for us poor college students. Look, I shouldn't stay on the phone, I'm being rude to my dinner companions. I just wanted to ask if you'd do me that favor. Thanks, Pops!"

"Anytime, young lady. I'll send you an email if there are any openings."

I hung up, and smiled at Michael and Tiffany. "He said he'll take a look and let us know."

Tiffany smiled at me. "Thanks, I really appreciate it!"

Michael gave me a sour look, since I'd made him look bad.

I found out more about the sour looks after dinner. Tiffany was going home, but I was joining the Spanish study group at the library. We walked Tiffany back to the apartment first, and they exchanged "Nice to meet yous" and "Thanks for dinners." Then Michael took my arm to walk me to the library. "You shouldn't have been promising Tiffany a job."

"I didn't promise anything," I protested. "I put out a question with someone who might know of openings. I told you before, it's called networking."

"Well, my father may be losing his job, so his company isn't likely to be doing any new hiring. Or, if they're doing any new hiring, it's because they're firing people like him, with years of experience, and hiring cheap college kids."

"Oh," I didn't know what to say to that. "I didn't know that. And your dad didn't tell me that."

"No, he wouldn't tell you that," he was glaring at me. "But that's the situation. He's been feeling depressed enough about his job lately, I'm sure he really needed you to make him think about it after he's come home from work for the day."

"I'm sorry, all right?" I was annoyed at him for being annoyed with me. "There's no way I was going to know that, is there?"

"I tried to discourage you from investigating that avenue," he pointed out.

"You could have told me the truth. You left me to think you were just being a dick about things, like you always are."

"I'm sure my father wouldn't want you to know that he might be out of a job soon. It's not exactly a pleasant prospect. It's not even for sure. The company is downsizing, but no one knows where they're going to make the cuts."

I felt bad for Pops, but now Michael had made it so that I couldn't admit it to him.

"Well, then, maybe he's got nothing to worry about."

Michael stopped to look at me. We were right outside the library. "My father, not worry? Have you ever known him to not be worrying? He makes up things to worry about when there isn't enough to worry about right in front of him."

"He does like to borrow trouble," I agreed. "Well, obviously I hope your dad gets to keep his job. And think, if he's able to find Tiffany a job, it will make him feel all powerful and important and well connected. So it could be good for his mental well-being."

Michael gave me a skeptical look, but said no more on the topic. He gave me my hug and kiss goodbye, and sent me on my way.

Nov 1

The problem of finding Tiffany a job keeps invading my thoughts. I'm grateful that my job allows me to go home for the summer but then they take me back every fall. I asked Tiffany if she's checked the student job board in the student union.

"There were some openings for nannies, but I don't think I'd be very good at that. I'm an only child, and I never did any babysitting. I don't know the first thing about kids," she admitted.

I have a really hard time imagining her wearing some drab clothes, baby vomit on her t-shirt, holding the hands of a toddler and a six-year-old while she tells them to look both ways before crossing the street. I'm not sure I've ever seen Tiffany in shoes that don't qualify as fuck-me-pumps. No wife would ever hire her to be under her roof, merely on her shoes alone.

"Yeah, there have got to be better jobs out there for you," I said. "Aren't there any jobs in your major?"

"There's lots of internships – all of them unpaid," she told me unhappily. "But I can't afford to work for free. I need a paying job."

Since Michael knows about my little side project, I made him brainstorm with me. "Come on, you're the big powerful executive, you must know other big, powerful executives from the Big Powerful Executives Club."

Michael gave me one of those looks of his. "You have a very interesting view of what it's like to run a company."

"And you are very stingy at sharing the details," I gave him a dirty look of my own.

That surprised him. "I'm stingy at sharing?"

"Ya think...? Instead of always talking to me as if I'm too little to understand, maybe one of these days you should experiment with treating me like an adult, and see what happens."

"That would be setting you up for failure. That would be ungallant of me."

I laughed at his choice of words. Ungallant? He was the soul of 'ungallant.' "I would say you would simply be acting true to your nature."

"In setting you up for failure? Nonsense. It's been my habit for almost half my life to look out for you."

"Well, at least you're very good at feeding me. That qualifies as looking out for me. And speaking of looking out for people – Tiffany!" I half stood up and waved. She was getting her change back from the cashier and picking up her tray. She saw me, and came over. "Hey, Lizzie. Nice to see you again, Michael."

"Hello, Tiffany." Michael moved his suit coat off the spare chair at our table. "Would you like to join us?" Darnedest thing about having other people around, Michael and I can't bicker as much when we have an audience.

"I'd love to, but my friends from my animation class are saving a seat for me. We're quizzing each other before our test this afternoon." She used her head to indicate a group of people at a table in the corner.

"How is the job hunt going?" he asked her.

"Since we had our discussion I put in a couple of job applications, but that's all I've had time for," she told us. "I'll have to go home for Christmas and find something then. I really hope I can find something full time up here next summer. I would love it if I didn't have to listen to my folks fighting all the time. Or if I have to go home, maybe I can find a night job, and avoid being home when they are."

I looked at Michael with my best puppy dog look after she walked away. "You aren't really going to condemn a girl to have to go home and listen to her parents fight all the time, are you?"

"Why is this suddenly my fault?" he asked.

"Because you're not helping me brainstorm ways we can help her get a job," I pointed out.

"You know, Tiffany's a big girl. She can find a job on her own. She hasn't asked you to help; has it ever occurred to you that maybe she doesn't want your help?"

"Everyone wants help," I contradicted him stubbornly.

"You know that's not true. You don't always want help. In fact, you usually don't want help. You want to figure things out for yourself."

There was a certain truth to what he was saying. Which of course I couldn't admit. "If you turn this into some story about how I wanted to tie my own shoelaces when I was six, I'm going to pull the laces off of the boots I'm wearing right now, and I'll strangle you with them," I threatened him.

"You see?" he wasn't distracted by my ploy. "You know I'm right."

Dec 7

Michael called me tonight for the first time in weeks. It's just as well, I've been plenty busy with getting my papers written and projects done. I should have texted or called or something to see if he was mad at me, but I was a little annoyed with him over his attitude about my wanting to help Tiffany. So I didn't mind that he wasn't calling me.

When I answered my phone, my first words were "Oh, so you're speaking to me again?"

"Since when am I not speaking to you?" he answered.

"Well, it's been weeks since I heard from you. I assumed you must be mad at me," I told him honestly.

"You're going through withdrawal, because I've been out of town?" he asked, but then he went on without waiting for my answer. "That's very sweet of you. I guess I should have let you know I had to go visit a job site out in Portland. It's probably had a significant impact on your grocery budget. Hard to plan if you don't know I'm not going to be around to feed you."

I was a little surprised by his lighthearted teasing answer. "Apology accepted. I've missed you, too, and not just the financial aid that comes attached to your presence."

"Well, I'm calling to make amends. I know you must be in the throes of final projects right now, but would you and Tiffany be able to spare the time to go to the Christmas Celtic Festival this weekend? I've got four tickets from one of my clients, and my friend Matt wants to go, but I can't get anybody else."

"Aw, gee, thanks, I'm your last resort, huh," I answered, although I was doing a happy dance on my side of the phone conversation. Before he could retract his offer, I continued, "I'd love to go! I'll ask Tiffany. I know she's got a lot to do, but she loves Irish music. And Guinness. I'm sure she'll find a way to make the time."

"Let me know as soon as you can, since it's only a couple days from now, and if she can't go, I can make some more phone calls."

That seemed sort of inconsistent. "I thought you said I was your last resort?"

"You said you were my last resort. I simply said I couldn't get anybody else," he corrected me.

"There's a difference?"

"Yes. I can always make more phone calls. My rolodex is pretty extensive."

"Oh, please tell me you don't really still use a rolodex," I laughed at him.

"And if I do?"

"Then I'm not sure if I can be seen in public with you, especially at Celtic Fest," I teased him back.

Of course I went, and of course Tiffany rearranged her schedule so that she could go, too. It was an irresistible offer! We were there with VIP passes, which we knew cost about a hundred dollars each. There was plenty of food and beverages included with our tickets, and special admission to several bars with live bands.

Matt turned out to be a pleasant companion. A little quiet, but I did pick up on the fact that he has kind of a snide sense of humor. I'd probably enjoy knowing him better, although he gravitated more toward Tiffany than me. And of course he talked more to Michael than he did to either of us. Having him and Tiffany with us prevented Michael and I from bickering all day long.

We had dinner in an Irish pub featuring karaoke. Tiffany and I looked over the list of available songs. I left to go to the bathroom, and when I came back, she was standing there, talking to her ex-boyfriend, Frank!

I hadn't seen Frank since our freshman year when they stopped dating somewhere in spring semester. I was going to join the conversation, but there was something about her body language that told me to stay away.

They were a distance from the karaoke list, so I went over to read it again. Frank could recognize me and say hi if he wanted to, or they could both ignore me if this conversation wasn't the sort that wanted to be interrupted.

I only caught snippets of it. He was saying "That's not my problem, now, is it?" And she was saying "But I thought that you wanted to." It didn't seem to be going well.

While I was wondering what to do, three girls got on stage and started singing "Boogie Woogie Bugle Boy" by the Andrews

Sisters. They were really good! Next thing I knew, Michael walked up to Tiffany and Frank. "Excuse me, but are you going to ask this lady to dance? If you're not, I'm going to."

"Be my guest," was the reply, and Michael took Tiffany by the hand and led her out on the floor in front of the stage.

I didn't know Michael knew how to swing dance! For that matter, I didn't know Tiffany knew how to swing dance. Or maybe she didn't, but Michael knew how to make her look good. Wow.

The two of them swayed, and twirled, and kicked. It was rather awesome to watch. Everyone hooted and clapped when they finished, probably as much for Michael and Tiffany as for the three girl singers. Michael and Tiffany clapped for the singers, the singers saluted them. Then they all left the stage.

Tiffany's face was flushed and smiling. I applauded as they walked over to me. "That was amazing! You guys looked great out there."

"Thanks! He made it seem so easy."

"It is easy," he said. "You follow well. Dancing is a matter of trusting your partner."

Matt came over to join us. He looked at Michael. "Show off. You said you were going to teach me to do some of that stuff."

Michael grinned at him. "Yes, I did. I'm sorry. I swear, I really will make the time to show you." A guy got on stage and started singing a slow Hugh Laurie song. "But maybe not right this minute."

"At least one of us should sing something," I pointed out. "There's no one else after this guy."

"Why don't you pick a song?" Michael asked me.

"I don't want to go up there and sing alone," I protested. "There's too many people watching."

"So, pick a song Tiffany can sing with you."

"If I pick a duet, will you sing it with me?" I asked him.

"Me? Sure. But I don't know a lot of current songs," he warned me.

"If they've got Boogie Woogie Bugle Boy, they must have other stuff old enough that even you'll know it," I goaded him.

"Gee, thanks," he answered, but he was smiling. He agreed to "Don't Go Breaking my Heart." Although then we argued about who sings it. I said it was John Travolta, he said it was Elton John. Tiffany pulled out her smart phone. Turns out we were both right. She found YouTube video of each, to prove it.

Dec 28

I was right about the law library, they asked me to catalogue the new materials over Christmas break! Woot, extra money! I started the day after I finished my last final, came home just for Christmas Eve and Christmas Day, then went back to school and back to my cataloguing. The campus was mostly deserted, and there was no one around to do anything for New Year's Eve, so I called Michael to see if he wanted to get together and do something.

"I would be happy to, but Carolyn and I are going to her sister's wedding that weekend," he explained.

"Carolyn your last ex-girlfriend Carolyn?" I was a little confused.

"That's the one."

"Are you guys getting back together again?" I don't know why, but I was really hoping this was not going to turn out to be the case.

"No, but her sister's soon-to-be-husband and I are close friends. I'm the one that introduced them. And Carolyn's new boyfriend has just rushed off to Kansas City because of a family emergency, so I'm filling in as her date."

Again, I was unaccountably displeased by this information. "You really want to spend New Year's Eve with the woman whom you recently referred to as 'that crazy bitch?' This doesn't sound like a good plan."

I was surprised by the candor of his answer. "Believe me, I'd much rather be spending it with you. But Randal is a close friend of mine, I can't miss his wedding. I'm sorry you're stranded out there. I promise, I'd come rescue you if I could."

"I know you would. Thanks, Michael."

Jan 2

So, I spent New Year's Eve with Anne and some of her sorority sisters who happen to live in town. It wasn't a bad time. Lots of Long Island Iced Teas. I haven't had one of those for a while, they are so good!

There was a guy there who was a dead ringer for Colin Firth. Anne kept trying to get me to go talk to him. After all, she knows my former obsession with all things Jane, and I haven't really talked to her about my epiphany. Either one of them: no Jane, and no men.

"Just go say hello. Brittany says he's not dating anybody at the moment. Well, she thinks he and his ex girlfriend are really broken up this time."

"No, thank you," I told her firmly. As firmly as anyone can tell anybody anything after three Long Islands. Or maybe it was four.

"I don't believe you're going to pass up the chance to meet a guy who looks just like Colin Firth," Anne obviously had no idea what to make of me. "What, are you getting a case of the shys?" Her face lit up. "I know, we can see if Brittany will set you up with him on a blind date."

This felt like we were venturing into some Jane Austen knockoff like Bridget Jones Diary. "No," I repeated. "Thank you, Anne, but I've sworn off guys this year. I had nothing but man troubles my first two years here. This semester I finally managed to get almost all As, because I refused to have anything to do with guys."

"What about that older guy, Mike, that you're constantly posting about on Facebook?" she asked. "I thought you might be dating him, but when you came to this party alone, I figured I was wrong."

Mike? Oh, she meant Michael. "I'm not dating him, he's a family friend. Kind of like an older brother, but more obnoxious," I explained.

Anne was looking at me skeptically. "Are you sure it's not dating? You're posting about him constantly."

"He has to be on campus a lot for his job."

"But he always makes time to see you when he's working?" She was giving me a penetrating look. "Are you sure he's not interested in you, and you're just being blind?"

I stared back at her. I tried to remember his exact words about wishing we could spend New Year's together. Then I wondered which one of us had picked the song "Don't go breaking my heart" to sing at the karaoke bar. Did I pick it, because he knew it? Or did he pick it, because he was trying to tell me something?

"That's why you're really not interested in Mr. Firth, over there, isn't it? It's because of this other guy, Mike."

"It's Michael, not Mike," I corrected her. And then I was out of things to say, so I downed the rest of my drink, declared that my glass was broken, and went to get a refill so it wasn't broken anymore.

Is that why Michael keeps taking me to dinner? He's interested in me? Does he really come around quite so frequently as Anne seems to think? When I got home I sat down and scrolled back over my Facebook posts. I guess I do seem to be posting an awful lot about having dinner with him somewhere. I thought I was bragging about going to all these fancy off campus places. Am I actually bragging that I'm there with him?

Dammit, I'd sworn off men this year. Now, here I am embroiling myself in another possibly romantic situation.

Feb 7

This afternoon I got further confirmation that I've been seeing an awful lot of Michael. I was wandering back to the apartment, conjugating Spanish verbs in my head, when Lon hailed me from one of the couches inside the lobby doors.

"I have a message for you from your boyfriend," he said, kind of stiffly.

I looked at him stupidly for a moment. "My what?"

"Your boyfriend was here a few minutes ago. He said his phone was dead, so he couldn't call or text you to tell you that he can't stick around for dinner tonight. He has a late meeting with a new client and he had to rush back to the office."

I was still having trouble with the boyfriend thing. "Wait – do you mean Michael?"

"If that's the guy you've been seeing the last couple of months," Lon said with a shrug. "The one you're always having dinner with."

"He's not my boyfriend," I protested. "He's an old friend of the family. We grew up together."

Lon wasn't looking at me anymore, his head was back at his computer screen. "Boyfriend, friend. The guy who kisses you goodnight all the time after he takes you out for dinner. He's not coming tonight. I've delivered my message, that's all I've got."

I stood there for a moment, stupidly staring at the top of Lon's head. He seemed angry. Or, upset. I wanted to make sure he knew that Michael wasn't a boyfriend. "How did he know that you knew me?"

"He was out here pacing around in front of the building waiting for you, so I told him you'd be along any minute now. He said he was in a big hurry, and asked if I'd tell you."

"Oh." I was at a loss for words again. "He's really not my boyfriend. He used to babysit me."

"More power to him, then."

Lon's posture over his computer was really telling me that he wanted me to get lost. I lingered a moment longer, wanting to say more, but right then Allie walked up. "Hey, Lizzie! Waiting for Michael?"

"No, he's not coming tonight." I headed to the elevator with her. I didn't want Lon hearing any more about Michael.

"That's a shame. I know how much you enjoy having dinner with him, even if he does aggravate you a lot."

"Yeah. It's kind of a love-hate relationship," I agreed. I was glad when the elevator doors closed. Lon definitely couldn't hear any more.

"My mom was asking if you two ever went out?" Allie asked.

"Go out, as in romantically involved? God, no. He's always too busy putting me down to say anything romantic."

"That's kind of what made us wonder. Tiffany says you guys do a lot of sparring, I thought maybe it was because you two are ex's."

"No, no such previous attachment," I said.

"So then maybe it's pent-up sexual tension?" she asked.

I stared at her a moment while she opened our door. This was the third time I was having this conversation in an awfully short period of time. "I hope not. That would be, like, incest."

"But you're not blood related, right?"

"No. Our parents went to college together. Michael was about to start college when I was born. I didn't, I couldn't, I mean - he's so old!" I interrupted myself.

Allie was positively smirking at me. "In exactly the same way Mr. Knightly was a lot older than Emma in that Jane Austen movie you made us watch with you our freshman year? Seems to me your 'love-hate relationship' looks a lot like that one."

Just then, Tiffany walked in. "Are you talking about Michael? Who cares how old he is? He's so good-looking. All the girls stared at him when we danced at the Christmas Celtic festival. You know," her voice dropped to a conspiratorial whisper, "older men have more experience in bed, and better bank accounts for taking girls out to dinner a whole bunch of times." She was smiling at me speculatively. Actually, so was Allie.

"Ew, are you seriously trying to talk me into dating him?" I asked.

"Well, if you don't go for him, maybe I will," Tiffany declared. "Is he seeing anybody right now?"

"No. He and his ex recently went to a wedding together, and he texted me to confirm he's feeling pretty glad that she's not his problem anymore." I remembered his texts to say Happy New Year, and he hoped my New Year's Eve was less lousy than his.

"Good to keep in mind." She dumped out her book bag and threw other things back into it. "I've got a group project to go work on. We're meeting for dinner before we start studying. Either of you want to join us?"

"Nah, I'm meeting Dale at the library, I just came home to grab my reading and change my shoes. I'll have to call my mother while I'm walking." Allie disappeared into her room, and came back out wearing a different sweater, lipstick, and these sweet platform shoes with little hearts cut into the leather on the sides.

"I still have a ton of Mexican history I have to read," I also turned down Tiffany's invitation. "I think we still have a few pizzas in the freezer."

"When my mom dropped off my laundry this morning, she brought us a bunch of groceries," Allie told me. "Check the fridge, everything with yellow labels is what we're supposed to eat first." Both my roomies waved goodbye and were back out the door.

Now I'm sitting here with this journal, looking out the window and procrastinating climbing the mountain of homework.

Michael Knox and Mr. Knightly. How did I not see it? When I was looking for a way to live out a Jane Austen story, it eluded me. When I gave up looking for a Jane Austen story, another one found me, anyway. Dammit! I'm done with Jane. I mean it. I want to move on with my life.

The preppy couple jogging down the street makes me think I should eat something healthier than pizza, something that involves a few veggies. I'll go see what Allie's mom brought us. She always worries about Allie eating too much junk food, and feeds all of us because she worries that if Tiffany and I eat pizza, we'll share with Allie. But I don't feel like boring healthy food. I could go get Chinese carryout. I wish I figured that out before I came all the way up here. Not that it's such a big deal, the Chinese place is just on the corner, but I feel squeamish about passing Lon again.

On the other hand, maybe I do want to bump into him. I could offer to get him dinner, too. Or maybe he would come along with me if I invite him.

I know I said no men this year, but suddenly I don't care.

Feb 8

Well no luck asking Lon to dinner last night. He was gone by the time I got back downstairs. I thought of knocking on his door, but I'd been up and down the elevator enough. I reminded myself I'd sworn off men, and I had a lot of reading to do, so I gave up and went to get my carryout.

It took me the most ridiculously long time to get my reading done. Not to mention my Spanish paper. How old do I have to be before I stop being a slave to my hormones? Amazing I can think about two different guys at the same time. There's Lon. I turned him down, I'm sorry I had, he told me he's glad I did. Since then he's been friendly, he's been cold, sometimes I think he likes me, sometimes, like this last time when he delivered Michael's message, I feel maybe he really doesn't.

Then there's Michael. Allie's right. My relationship to him is almost exactly Emma Woodhouse's relationship with Mr. Knightly. Both are older and critical. But he picked on her because he was in love with her. He'd been in love with her since she was thirteen.

Is that how Michael feels about me? If Emma and Knightly's quarrels were an expression of sexual tension, is the same true for me and Michael? It is sort of sexy to think that maybe that's the case. Maybe I'd feel differently if he confessed to me that he loves me. Will he ever do such a thing? If the last two years of my life are any indication, it seems very unlikely.

The more I wonder, the more confused I'm getting. The more confused I am, the worse my Spanish is becoming. I tried to put this down and finish my Spanish paper - I actually found myself looking up the conjugation of the verb "to be," because I had no idea how to say "I am." This is not going to be my most stellar Spanish paper.

Now I'm sitting here, trying to proofread it, still thinking about the possibility of Michael being my Mr. Knightly. Is it possible? Is it probable? Is it the craziest thing I'd ever heard of? I don't know. I do know I can't wait to see him again, so I can start getting some answers.

Feb 16

I haven't heard from him for a week, so I decided to take action and texted Michael.

> Hey, dumbass, next time don't forget to charge your phone. I hope your new client appreciated the sacrifice you made, giving up the chance to have dinner with me.

I have to sound like myself, after all. He wrote back about an hour later.

> Well, stop texting me so much, then. You're murder on my battery.

I grinned as I wrote back,

> It's not me, it's the GPS. You're using it to navigate, aren't you? That eats up battery like nobody's business.

It took him another hour to answer.

> Guilty as charged. Now stop texting me, I've got a lot of meetings today. I'll call you when I'm on campus again. Just so you know, it's not going to be for at least two or three weeks.

Maddening! How on earth am I supposed to figure out what's going on, if I can't see him?

Mar 24

Well, my wait turned out to be much longer than I'd dreamed, but it's over. I got to see him today. It's his Dad's 60th birthday, which coincides with spring break, so his family decided to go to New Orleans and throw this really big blowout birthday party.

My parents picked me up, and the five of us had a lot of fun on the drive there. Both David and Wendy are taking Spanish in school now, so we are having fun confounding our parents by speaking Spanish as much as we can. It's like having a secret code.

Michael flew in today, just in time for the party. He gave me a hug and a kiss when we saw each other, but I couldn't detect any particular significance in either. It was the same hug and kiss he gives me after all our dinners, same as all the other hugs and kisses going back as far as I can remember. After we said hello, he didn't exactly stick around near me. But then, there were lots of people around. My parents were there, his parents were there of course, the other two college friends were there, all of us kids were there along with all kinds of other extended family.

They rented a picnic shelter in this gorgeous park. Grills were going with hot dogs and hamburgers, and potato salad and coleslaw and every other picnic salad that you tend to see mostly in the summer. I do wonder how many generations will have to pass before people stop making salads that incorporate Jell-o.

They had the lawn games out. We played croquet, badminton, and cornhole. Someone even brought a set of lawn darts, the kind they don't sell anymore because the tips are pointy and someone must have sued a toy company because they didn't know that toddlers are very likely to run in front of people playing lawn darts if you don't keep an eye on them.

We tried to keep rotating the teams, playing girls against boys, the oldest against the youngest, dividing by family relations, and by picking numbers between 1 and 100. Nonetheless, some people always ended up on the same teams, and some people never got to be on the same team. Unfortunately, I kept ending up on the same team as Josie.

Josie is the daughter of another friend from the college clique with Pops and my dad. She is almost exactly the same age as me, so everyone said that wow, we would just have to be best friends. They've been shoving her down my throat since we were in diapers. I can't say I appreciate the favor. I pick my own friends, thanks, and Josie isn't my type. I had been so glad that she went skiing at Aspen over New Year's two years ago, when our families threw the big New Year's Eve party.

Josie is one of those people who gets on your nerves quickly. She's always the victim, always talking, always the attention whore. There isn't enough attention in the whole world to make her happy. People never treat her the way she wants to be treated, and somehow it's never her fault when things don't work out. Sometimes she tells these stories about herself, and I have trouble knowing what parts are true, and what parts aren't. It's always clear that some significant portion of her stories are fabrication.

Josie was in fine form at the picnic. The other team was always cheating. She pouted when everyone else wanted to play lawn darts, we had to play badminton first because that's what she wanted. Then she chatted all through croquet about how awful her ex-boyfriend was, and how she wasn't sure if she was safe in her own apartment since they broke up.

"Are you talking about the guy who bought you a car?" I asked. I was having trouble listening to her any more. "Maybe he's breaking in to get the car keys back."

"Oh, no he's letting me keep the car," she told me.

"Well, in that case, he doesn't sound all that awful," I observed.

She tossed her pretty head. She has this technique for tossing her head that makes her boobs jiggle. She has a lot of boob to jiggle, and always wears tight low cut tops to show off her boobs. I doubt there's a man alive who could tell you what color her eyes are.

"You wouldn't understand. You've never dated anyone. When you get into a relationship someday, you'll find out for yourself that men are very complicated."

Complicated, my ass. Here was a girl who reduced men to their basest component by perpetually flashing her admittedly very nice tits at them, and she wanted to give herself airs? "Well, that's why I'm not in a hurry to jump into any sort of complications," I answered. "I have a job, so I don't need to sell my body in order to get a car. Eventually I'll buy my own."

"I can't believe you just called me a whore," her big blue eyes filled with tears. "You really meant that. That's really what you think of me, you think I'm a whore." She threw down her croquet mallet. "I don't suppose you want a whore on your team. You can finish without me." She walked away, still tossing her hair and jiggling her boobs.

"You weren't exactly helping our team much," I called after her. "Now maybe we won't lose as badly."

The third member of our team was Michael. "Nice going," he said to me. "Did you really have to provoke her until she quit?"

"One could easily argue that she's the one who provoked me," I pointed out.

"You could show a little more compassion," he chastised me. "She's recently broken up with a boyfriend, and had to move back home with her parents. It's got to be very humiliating, after being out on your own, to have to return to your childhood bedroom."

"Are you shitting me?" I laughed at his portrayal. "Moving in with a boyfriend does not equal being out on your own. She only changes whom she's sponging off."

"I don't think you're being very fair to her," he was looking at me accusingly.

"Why don't you butt out? I've got my own opinion of her, and those of us who have not been blessed with a Y chromosome have a unique ability to see more than her tits."

"Did you ever stop to think that maybe having a gorgeous body is more of a curse for her than a blessing?" he was glaring at me. "You could stand to be a little less judgmental of people." He put away his croquet mallet and walked off.

I looked at his retreating back. "Well, tell you what, you show yourself to be a good judge of people, and I'll listen to what you have to say when making character assessments. But don't expect me to change my opinion that she's a skanky whore, and I have the right to call bullshit on her when she's sneering at me because I've never had a boyfriend." He couldn't hear me, but I said it anyway. It did make me feel better.

Michael and I didn't talk for the rest of the picnic. I don't know if he was specifically avoiding me. I assume he was. I was certainly avoiding him. We didn't even say goodbye. He wasn't around when we left. He had a rental car, so I couldn't tell if he was still in the park somewhere, or if he'd gone when we all said our goodbyes to Pops and took our leave. Josie was nowhere to be seen either; maybe they'd gone off together. She can move in with him, next, and then he will find out for himself what a mooch she is.

Apr 11

It's been almost three weeks, and he finally called me today. Tiffany and I ran into each other walking through the square, and were walking back to our apartment together, when my phone rang. It was Michael. I wasn't sure if I wanted to answer.

"Oh, answer it," Tiffany told me. I'd told her all about the picnic. "He probably wants to take you someplace really nice to apologize."

So I hit the answer icon. "Hey."

"Hey, yourself. I'm on campus, if you want dinner. Not that I'm accusing you of being a freeloader like Josie, or anything."

That was exactly the wrong thing to say. "No, I have a paper due in the morning that I have to work on," I told him. I looked at Tiffany. "But Tiffany would love to have dinner with you, if you are feeling charitable and want to help feed a starving college student."

They both talked at once. "Sure, I'll come by and pick up Tiffany," Michael was saying, while Tiffany said, "Lizzie! How do you know I don't already have plans?"

I put my phone on mute. "Well, do you want an off-campus experience with a guy with deep pockets, or not?"

She looked at me sheepishly. "Yes."

I took my phone off mute. "You want to meet her in the lobby? What time?"

"I should be there in ten minutes."

I looked at Tiffany. "Ten minutes?" I asked her.

"Sure," she answered. "Um, wait, tell him fifteen."

"Take your time," I told Michael, "It's gonna take about fifteen minutes for us to get back to our apartment, and she has to dump off her books." That was a lie. We were walking into the building. But I knew what was going through her head. She was going to change her clothes and throw on a little bit more makeup. Tiffany could have been a sorority girl. I haven't seen anyone as conscientious about makeup since I roomed with Anne. That's part of why I can't pledge to a sorority. Besides the money part, I don't routinely wear makeup.

"Okie dokie. I'll see her in fifteen, then." He hung up.

I smiled at Tiffany. "You got yourself a date."

"Does he actually think it's a date? Or am I a charity case to him?" she asked me.

"That depends," I pointed out as we got in the elevator. "If he enjoys your company so much he is inspired to invite you to dinner again without my having to intercede, someday this will be looked upon as a first date. If he simply tolerates you for my sake, or he sees this as some sort of apology to me for being an ass at the picnic, then it's not really a date." I unlocked the door, and stepped aside for Tiffany to dash in first. As I guessed, she threw off her t-shirt and pajama pants, pulled on a cute little dress, strapped on these cute wedges, freshened up her makeup and ran a brush through her hair.

She came to my door. "Will I do?"

I looked her over. "You're too sexy for words. He doesn't deserve you. Have a good time."

She waved, and ran off.

I pulled out my Spanish art textbook and my notebook, figuring I'd work on my paper here for a while, since I didn't want to see Michael. I wasn't that hungry yet, anyway.

I feel happier than I've felt for some time, and I realize it's because I've "gotten rid" of Michael. He's a psychological vampire. He's always criticizing. It is mentally and emotionally exhausting, being under attack all the time. Always having to be on the defense. Having to explain my actions, and sometimes even my lightest utterances. He would destroy the ego of anyone without a very healthy sense of self-worth. Most people say ego like it's a bad thing, but having no ego whatsoever is no good, either.

He will always be an old friend of the family, but I will be a much healthier and happier person if I don't see him week in and week out. If Tiffany wants him, she can have him.

I thought about Emma and Mr. Knightly. Mr. Knightly was always a critical cranky jerk, and then suddenly she figures out that she's in love with him, and he suddenly stops being critical and says he's in love with her. See, once again, Jane is wrong. People don't suddenly change like that. They don't suddenly own up to their own faults, and say "I've humiliated you and lectured you, and you've borne it like no other woman in England." Guys never get around to admitting when they're cranky jackasses. It's simply not true to human nature.

Apr 11 Part two

I'm writing this four hours later, because I still can't concentrate.

After Tiffany left, I threw a frozen pizza in the oven, studied some more, and then decided to move to the rooftop. There are some nice little tables and chairs up there, and I wanted to sit in a different position for a while. Besides, the weather looked gorgeous outside my window. I was tired of being indoors.

It turns out there was a party on the rooftop. There were a whole bunch of guys, and a handful of women, and music, and balloons, and a banner that said "Congratulations."

Someone handed me a margarita. I hadn't known what it was, since everything was in red solo cups. But after I took a drink, expecting Mountain Dew since it was poured out of a 2-liter of Mountain Dew, I knew better.

"Oh, that's good. I needed a good caffeine hit, since I still have studying to do tonight. But this is even better." The guy who poured me the drink was named Paul, I think. I've seen him around, but we've never really talked. There are a lot of people living in an apartment building, and a whole lot of people you sort of pass in the hall or lobby or elevator without getting to know them.

"I had a professor in English Comp who told us that when you can't seem to get anything down on paper because the internal censor keeps interfering, give him a shot and tell him to go to sleep for a while." Paul grinned at me. "I couldn't believe a professor would be advocating underage drinking. Of course, when the class compared notes, most of us weren't exactly alcohol virgins."

I laughed at his turn of phrase. "That's a very apt expression." I pointed my half empty glass at the congratulations banner and the balloons. "So what's the occasion?"

"You mean you're not actually invited to this party?"

"If I say no, I just came up here to study, are you going to take away my margar – my Mountain Dew?" I asked.

"Well, no, I'll let you keep it," he laughed. "Lon did warn me when I suggested we throw the party up here that this is a public space, and we might get a couple of party crashers."

"Are you his roommate, then?" I felt kind of stupid, you'd think I'd have known at least that much about him. I spotted Lon now, standing with a little group of people.

"Yeah. I'm the lucky SOB who gets to say I know the guy who gets to go to NASA this summer."

I wasn't following the conversation at all. "I'm sorry, what?"

"That's why we're throwing this party. Lon just got accepted to do an internship at NASA. He leaves as soon as finals are over." He turned around when a couple of other girls brought him their solo cups for refills, then he poured the remaining half a cup into my glass.

"Thanks," I smiled at him. "Wow. That's amazing news," I said, a trifle too loudly. Lon had moved over to the makeshift bar behind Paul, and I was trying to make sure he could overhear me. "So is he going to Texas or Florida?" I was proud of myself for knowing that's where NASA is located. When I glanced over to see if Lon noticed us talking about him, though, he was gone.

"They don't really do research at either of those places. Cape Canaveral is where they launch missions, and the Johnson Space Center is where Mission Control is located," Paul explained.

I was disappointed. Here I thought I'd get credit for knowing that NASA was based in those places, and instead I get to look stupid for not knowing where they send interns. "So where will he be going?"

"Cleveland, Ohio."

"Cleveland? That's kind of a shame," I commented. "Not exactly glamorous."

"Glamorous enough, if you're working for NASA," Paul pointed out.

To end the awkward lull in our conversation that happened at that point, I asked him, "So what's it like to have Lon as a roommate? He seems so serious all the time."

"Serious? Lon? Well, I guess so. He's really funny, it's hard to see past his taste for practical jokes. But you're right, when he's not showing us how to blow up outhouses, he's usually studying. He's really, really smart."

Out of the corner of my eye, I saw Lon brush past again. He was now standing behind me. I kept my eyes glued on his roommate's face.

"He asked me out at the very beginning of our freshman year," I told Paul. "I wasn't in a good place to be dating anybody at the time, so I said no. I'm sorry I turned him down. He seems like a great guy." I made sure my voice was loud enough so that Lon would be able to hear me even though I had my back to him.

"Yeah, he is. He's probably going to own his own spaceship company or something like that someday. Our entire fraternity is going insane with jealousy over the NASA thing."

"I bet." I looked around casually, like I was surveying the party. "This is so much fun, but I really should go back to studying." Darn it, Lon probably hadn't overheard me at all, he was on the far side of the roof now. "Since your party has the roof hopping, I'll just go back to study in my room. He seems kind of busy right now, would you tell him that Lizzie says congratulations?"

"I'll do that," Paul promised.

"Thanks," I said. "And thanks so much for the drink."

"No problem," he said, and then he went to open another Mountain Dew bottle.

Apr 13

Well, Tiffany's dinner with Michael went well. They're officially dating now! The funny thing is, deep down in my heart I expected to not be okay with this. I know I said 'good riddance,' but there's a difference between saying something out of bravado, and really meaning it.

It turns out, I really meant it. I am not Emma, Michael is not Mr. Knightly. Emma was hit by a wave of terror when she realized she might lose Mr. Knightly to Harriet Smith. When Tiffany came back from dinner, hours later, singing, her eyes shining, and she told me he asked for her number and asked if he could take her out again, all I could do was laugh.

"Okay, you're making me nervous, why are you laughing?" she asked.

"I don't know why. I'm happy for you. I'm happy for both of you. I hope it works out," I told her.

"Are you sure? I was a little afraid to tell you, I thought that maybe you had a thing for him yourself, even though you said otherwise."

"What, are you calling me a liar?" I was still laughing.

"Well, no, but you know sometimes we lie to ourselves."

I gave her a hug. "Michael is an old friend. Nothing more. He's always harping on how he's known me all my life, and changed my diapers, and stuff that goes back to when I was two years old. He's never going to let me grow up. I don't want to be with someone who is never going to let me grow up."

A worried look crossed her face. "Do you think it's going to be a problem that I'm so much younger? I'm only two months older than you."

I thought about it before I answered. "No, I don't think this is about being younger. He doesn't have a history with you. He has a history with me. It's not because he's old enough to be my dad, it's that he changed my diapers, and remembers my first word, and carried me on his shoulders so I could see parades better, as if he was actually my dad. We can't change our history. I don't think either one of us would want to. It's just not that kind of relationship."

There it is. It's just not that kind of relationship.

I lay awake last night, turning it over and over in my mind. How could Emma suddenly fall in love with Mr. Knightly, who had a habit of scolding her like a child? Emma's own father was such an indulgent parent, Mr. Knightly was really a second father to her. The strict one who criticized her behavior. How does one jump from father figure to lover? This strikes me as increasingly implausible. It certainly doesn't hold true for me in my life. I don't have any daddy issues. I don't want a father figure for a boyfriend. And I'm not sure if Emma was being true to character, either.

This isn't a good way of keeping my vow of no men this year. On the other hand, all along I haven't been thinking of Michael as a man, so I haven't been breaking my vow. That tells me something, right there.

May 15

I can't believe it's finals time already! This year, though, I don't feel quite so out of control. I'm not going into chemistry finals, knowing I'm going to bomb them, or turning in photography projects that inspire my teachers to tell me I just "don't have the eye" for this stuff. While I'm writing in Spanish, I think in Spanish. I'm not thinking in English and then translating it. I think I'm even going to ace the Mexican history class, even though I've never been a big one for history.

As much as I love the sweet spot in the library where my friends still bump into each other, I had too much studying to do to be distracted by talking. So I steered around that part, and wandered up an extra floor. There are tables and chairs and clusters of comfy chairs in front of the big windows, filled with people madly working away. I wasn't sure I was going to be able to find an empty spot, but I thought I'd check.

And there, in the corner, I spotted Lon. He had his feet on an ottoman, his laptop across his legs, and there was an empty chair next to him.

"Hey," I said softly, not sure if I should interrupt him or not. He was typing away madly. "Could you stand a study buddy?"

He was a really fast typist. He was so into his work, I don't think he heard me. He eventually realized I was standing there. "Oh, hello."

"Hi. May I join you?" I pointed at the empty chair next to him.

Lon glanced at the chair, then back up at me. "Suit yourself."

This made me hesitate. "If I'm too much of a disruption, just say so."

"Only if you plan on talking to me instead of studying," he pointed out.

This made me shut up and sit down. I opened my book and my notes, and read everything over, but I wasn't absorbing anything. I was too aware of his being next to me.

After about an hour, he stopped typing and closed his notebook. "So, are you getting any work done? I'm not."

His question surprised me. "No, I'm not," I admitted. "Why aren't you getting your work done? I haven't said a word to you since I sat down, and you've been typing the whole time."

"You're still a distraction. You have very nice legs, and you smell like vanilla or something."

I was totally floored by his compliments. "It's lavender and honey," I stammered.

"It's nice." He looked at me speculatively for a moment. I don't know why, but I had to work hard not to squirm under his gaze. Then he smiled. "I did hear what you wanted me to overhear back at my party," he told me.

"About congratulating you for getting into NASA?" I tried to remember what I'd said. "I'm very happy for you. I'm sure you'll be brilliant and impress them all."

He was still giving me a look that I couldn't define. "I'm talking about your retroactive acceptance of my invitation to go out with me. Do you really regret having said no when I asked you?"

"Duh!" The word was out of my mouth before I could stop it. I really would have preferred to say something a little more articulate. I remembered what I'd told his roommate. "I do think you're a really great guy, and I'm sorry I hadn't said yes when you asked me out." Now it was my turn to give him a look. "You told me not that long ago that you were glad I'd said no."

I couldn't believe my eyes, he was actually blushing! "Can we forget we had that conversation? I hadn't slept for two days trying to get a big project done, it wasn't going well, and I was a jackass to just about everyone I saw that day."

How completely different from Michael, who has never apologized to me once in his life for being a jackass to me all the time! "Well, you're right, I'm not a straight A student, and we don't have a lot in common. I can't talk to you about math and physics. If it matters to you, now that I've found my stride and declared my major in Spanish, my grades are a lot better. I've found something I'm actually good at."

Lon was blushing harder now. "See what I mean about being a jackass? I'm so sorry I said that." He cleared his throat. "I was absolutely wrong about the math and physics thing. I talk about those things all day long, I don't need to talk about them in my free time, too. My mom's a nurse, and my dad works in finance, they get along fine without dad knowing the names of all the muscles and bones, or mom knowing how mutual funds work."

"My parents own a nursing home, they never talk about anything else except their nursing home," I said. "Come to think of it, dinner conversations would be much more interesting if they knew how to talk about anything else."

"Would you be willing to go to dinner with me, and let's see if we can find anything to talk about? I promise no math and physics, and, I should warn you, I don't speak any Spanish. So neither of us knows anything about the other's area of expertise."

"I would love to go to dinner with you," I had this big, warm, squishy feeling in my stomach as I accepted his invitation. "But what do we do if this goes well? You're heading for Cleveland for the summer, and I need to do a semester abroad next fall as a Spanish major."

"Shall we just take this one step at a time?" I liked the way he was looking at me. He was giving me a kindly smile, like the one he gave me when I got caught in the rain and he walked me home. "If you have to come visit me in Cleveland, and I have to come visit you in Spain or Mexico or Argentina or something, that doesn't sound like a bad thing to me."

"You'd do that?" I couldn't imagine a guy going to a foreign country just to come see me.

"I like to travel." He gave me this impish sort of smile. "I've never been to any Spanish-speaking countries, so I'm hoping this dating thing works out with you."

"Just so you can have a free place to crash?" I was smiling back.

"Fine, call me an opportunist."

I realized he was leaning toward me a little, and I started blushing. "Well, I've never been to Cleveland, so I guess I'm hoping this dating thing works out, too."

My heart was beating crazily, and I was still blushing, and at the same time I was leaning toward him a little, too. We were close enough I could smell his scent. I like the way he smells. Like soap and Speed Stick.

He tilted his head while he examined my red face. "I know this is taking things out of order, we're supposed to do dinner, then a movie or something, and then I ask this, but may I kiss you?"

I stopped breathing entirely. "I thought you'd never ask."

First kisses aren't anything like they are in the movies. There's no tongue, no open mouths, not a lot of smashing your faces together. It's much better than that.

May 19

So dinner with Lon was delightful. He likes as many different kinds of Asian cuisines as I do, which we discovered while we plowed through some of the best sushi I've ever had. We found we had plenty to talk about, even though I can't talk about physics and he can't speak in Spanish. We found out both of us like Star Wars AND Star Trek, and we don't see the point in pitting one against the other. They're both good.

AND - Lon has seen EVERY movie ever made of a Jane Austen book. He says I'm going to get along famously with his mom and his sister. He's the one - not me- who compared our relationship (thus far) to Anne and Captain Wentworth.

"I hope your parents aren't going to be puzzled when they find out I want to date their daughter." We were sitting across the table from each other, and he was holding my hand in both of his.

"As in, 'Anne, you want to marry Anne? Whatever for?' " I laughed.

"Exactly."

"That's probably exactly what my brother and sister will say. If we're really lucky, my mother will start by asking when she gets to have grandbabies."

He kissed the back of the hand he had been toying with. "One step at a time?"

"One step at a time," I agreed.

He took me home after dinner, and immediately started his drive to Cleveland. He got out of his car to kiss me goodbye. It was a bit more wild than our first kiss, and I feel a little bit bad about it. We ended up denting the fender of his Porsche.

So, maybe Jane knew what she was talking about, after all…

ABOUT THE AUTHOR

Jeanette Watts normally writes historic fiction set in Pittsburgh, but when she had the idea to write Jane Austen Lied to Me on the drive home from the Jane Austen Festival, she found it too irresistible to ignore.

When she isn't writing, she teaches Vintage ballroom dance and belly dance, sews quilts, costumes, and dolls, and wishes she had more time to read.